The Sheik's Siren

The Del Taran

Elizabeth Lennox

Copyright 2022
ISBN13: 9798796526439
All rights reserved

This is a work of fiction. Names, characters, businesses, places, events, and incidents are either the product of the author's imagination or used in a fictitious manner. Any resemblance to actual persons, living or dead, or actual events is purely coincidental. Any duplication of this material, either electronic or any other format, either currently in use or a future invention, is strictly prohibited, unless you have the direct consent of the author.

Table of Contents

Chapter 1   1

Chapter 2   13

Chapter 3   17

Chapter 4   21

Chapter 5   30

Chapter 6   44

Chapter 7   57

Chapter 8   71

Chapter 9   81

Chapter 10	85
Chapter 11	91
Chapter 12	96
Chapter 13	99
Chapter 14	103
Chapter 15	109
Chapter 16	111
Chapter 17	129
Epilogue	137
Postepilogue	139
Excerpt from "The Sheik's Siren"	142

Chapter 1

The harsh sounds of multiple cars crashing and glass breaking pulled his eyes away from the report he'd been reading. Looking out the window, Sheik Zantar Al Abouss glanced around, feeling the sudden tension of his guards as they all went on high alert, trying to figure out why traffic had come to a sudden halt. His armored SUV was not part of the accident, but there were four cars ahead that were badly mangled.

"I'll see what's going on," one of the guards said, stepping out of the vehicle. The man stepped onto the sidewalk and looked around, moving several feet down the road.

Once again, Zantar looked out the window and…couldn't believe his eyes! A woman was on the beach in the most bizarre pose he'd ever seen. In fact, he wasn't even sure how she'd gotten her arms and legs into that pose! Her legs were in the air, her hands down in the sand. Her head was…he wasn't sure. Slowly, her long, sexy legs lowered to the sand and she stood up, her very delectable derriere leading the way.

The guard who had stepped out of the SUV to investigate the traffic jam came back with an irritated huff. "It's the woman!" he snarled, jerking his thumb towards the woman behind him. "She distracted the drivers up ahead. In fact, the four drivers of the crashed vehicles are standing on the side of the road, watching the woman." The guard huffed and looked over his shoulder, even tilting his head slightly as the woman in question moved into a different yoga position. "What the hell is she doing?"

Zantar threw back his head, laughing at the beautiful scenario. The woman was merely exercising, completely oblivious to the chaos around her. She had no idea that the relatively conservative country of Skyla wasn't ready for a woman in skintight clothing to be moving in that manner. His country of Citran was a bit more liberal, but the woman's figure was enticing enough that the men in his country would probably have the same reaction.

Even as he watched, the woman centered herself, put her hands in front of her chest, palms together, eyes closed and went very still. No one moved. It seemed as if no one even breathed as everyone watched…silently waiting. A brief moment later, the lovely woman sighed and nodded, her hands lowering to her lap.

Entranced, Zantar's laughter was long forgotten as the woman stood up, lifted her face to the early morning sunshine, and smiled! A second later, she threw her hands up in the air as if she were somehow trying to hug the sunshine! Or the waves? He wasn't sure. Maybe both.

A moment later, she turned and his breath caught in his throat as he stared at her lovely face. She pulled the band out of her hair and the ocean breeze pulled the strands higher, lifting the soft, brown locks into the air, swooping it all around her face. She wasn't bothered. The woman simply pulled her hair out of her eyes and bent down, picking up a long skirt. She wrapped it around her tiny waist, then rolled up her yoga mat, stuffed it into a bag and walked up the beach to the sidewalk.

Zantar was captivated. Completely enraptured by the beauty of the woman. No, not just her beauty. He'd been with many beautiful women over the years. It wasn't just her full, soft lips or the delicate line of her jaw. It wasn't her now-covered derriere or her full breasts, hidden by a loose shirt, yet still visible when she bent down to slide sandals onto her feet.

There was something more, something different and alluring about the woman. He wanted her. Zantar knew that his desires were impossible. He was only here visiting Sklya because of some mysterious issue that the Sheik of Skyla and the Sheik of Silar needed to discuss with him. The fact that both men had asked him to visit and that the meetings would include three of the most powerful leaders in their region was enough for Zantar to realize that something significant was happening.

Pulling his eyes away from the woman, Zantar tried to focus back on his reports. He didn't bother to glance at his watch. He didn't have time, and yet, a moment later, he reached for the door handle and stepped out of the vehicle. His guards instantly moved to surround him but he waved a hand, silently telling them to spread out as he moved towards the woman walking along the beach. It wasn't as if his guards could move the SUVs. The four-car pileup ensured that the people on the street weren't going anywhere. The traffic was completely snarled now. It was going to take several tow trucks and the police taking statements to get this situation cleared out before he could be on his way. He might as well put the delay to good use.

"Good morning," he called out.

Instantly, the woman stopped, her loose-limbed walk halting as she stared up at him from six feet away.

"Who are you?" the woman demanded, squinting up at him now that the sun was higher over the horizon.

"You may call me Zantar," he replied, sliding his hands into his pockets to keep them from reaching out to pull her closer. She was even more stunning close up. Her light blue eyes were surrounded by thick, dark lashes. Her skin was tanned, but he suspected that was due to the sun rather than heredity. And her lips...damn her mouth was full and sensuous, wide and curving up at the corners even as she looked at him warily.

She hesitated for a moment, her mouth opening slightly as if she were as caught up in the awareness of him as he was with her. Good, he thought, even more intrigued.

"Good morning, Zantar," she said softly. She took another step closer, then halted. "You're very tall!"

He lifted a dark eyebrow. "And you're very dangerous," he replied.

Her eyes widened. "I am?" Those lips curved into a smile. "I think I like the idea of being dangerous." She stepped closer again. "How am I dangerous? Do I look mysterious?"

He chuckled, shaking his head, but he pulled one hand out of his pocket as he pointed behind her at the crash site, two of the men still standing on the sidewalk watching her.

She looked over her shoulder, then her head swiveled back to him. "The accident?"

"Yes, *eazizi*," he replied, his voice deeper now, as he realized that she was unaware of the impact she had on men. On him!

Her head tilted slightly and it seemed as if she were concentrating. "That means..." she pressed her lips together for a moment, then shook her head. "I'm sorry. I've only started to learn your language. I'm not familiar with that word."

His lips curled slightly and he was suddenly startled to discover that she was American. They'd been speaking in English this whole time but he'd been so distracted by her mouth and those blue eyes, he hadn't even realized it. He should have assumed her country of origin based on the casual style of her hair and the loose feel of her clothing. Perhaps he would have noticed those details, but her eyes...they were quite startling. And her mouth was wide and full and...luscious.

"Where are you off to?" he asked, ignoring her question about the translation. He'd called her "my dear", and even he was surprised by the intimacy implied by that term.

Her confusion dissipated and her features brightened as she smiled up at him. "I'm going to grab a cup of coffee at that small coffee shop over there," she explained, pointing towards the corner shop with green umbrellas and metal chairs. "And then I have to hurry off to work."

He contemplated her for a moment, his eyes glancing behind her once again. There was no movement at the crash site, so he made a snap decision. "I will join you for coffee," he announced.

The woman's body seemed to jerk slightly, but her smile brightened even more. "You will? Well, I'm so glad that I invited you to join me then!" she replied with a teasing smile.

Zantar grunted slightly, not sure how he felt about her teasing. For some reason, he liked it. But he didn't want to like it. She was...cute. And sexy. And enticing. It was startling that she already felt comfortable enough to tease him. Or was that just part of her personality? For some reason, he didn't like that thought. He preferred thinking that this fascinating woman...what? Was his? He'd just met her!

However, when she started walking again, her stride long and confident and her blue eyes twinkling up at him, he felt a possessive surge rise up inside of him.

It was just coffee, he reminded himself. And yet, when she stepped closer as they walked along the sidewalk, his hand moved to the small of her back.

Faye felt his hand and looked up at him, startled by the intense heat emanating from the man. His hand scorched her skin through her shirt but...that was impossible, right?

"I'm Faye, by the way," she told him.

He looked down at her, his dark eyes sharp, seeming to take in details that she knew nothing about. "That is a very pretty name, Faye," he replied.

He pronounced her name as if it were a lullaby. Something melted inside of her and she smiled up at him. This day just kept getting better and better, she thought. "Why did you imply that I was the cause of the accident back there?" she said, gesturing absently with her hand to the area that was now behind them.

"You were doing yoga on the beach," he explained, his voice deep and gravelly.

She chuckled. "Let's just examine this for a moment," Faye said, stopping and smiling when he stopped as well. "You're saying that I'm the cause of the accident. And yet, I was minding my business over there on the beach. The subjects of the accident are the four men who weren't paying attention to where they were going."

"And yet, you were the distraction."

Again, Faye shook her head. "*They* were distracted. *I* was not distracting them. I was not an active participant in their distraction. You are saying that men are too weak to concentrate. If that's true, if men are too easily distracted, then perhaps they should not be allowed to drive."

He didn't respond to that and Faye's features brightened even more. Finally, he grunted, and Faye wasn't sure if that was acceptance of her argument or a dismissal because her comments didn't fall into place with the normal arguments that women should always cover up to avoid being a "temptation" to men.

She squinted up at him, trying to translate that sound. "Were you a bear in a past life?" she asked.

Her question clearly startled him, and she might have laughed at his odd expression but he took her arm as they crossed the street. With any other man of her acquaintance, she would have been peeved at his possessively protective gesture. But for some reason, his hand on her arm felt good. It felt right. Hot, almost, singeing, yes. But also right.

The man named Zantar waited until they were on the other side of the street before responding, telling Faye that her safety was his main concern. That was sort of sweet, she thought.

"Explain your bear question. I don't understand your meaning," he growled, his eyes scanning the area ahead of them.

She grinned but her attention was caught by Efin, the waiter who was currently waving at her from the café. "You're going to love this coffee!" she whispered, hurrying along the sidewalk. As soon as she stepped up into the fenced off area of the coffee shop, she threw her arms around Efin, then stepped back. "Oh, isn't today a glorious day?"

Efin smiled, but glanced nervously behind her. A moment later, he focused his attention back on Faye, his greeting becoming more teasing now. "Faye, you say that every morning is glorious."

She laughed, bouncing a bit on the balls of her feet, her energy high this morning. "Well, every morning is beautiful, isn't it?" She twirled around, her wrap-around skirt lifting to float around her legs. She lifted her face up to the sky and smiled, absorbing the warmth of the sunshine. "It's just amazing here! We don't get sunshine like this back in Georgia! It's hot and humid but this..." she sighed and lifted her arms up. "This dry heat is amazing!"

Efin laughed, rolling his eyes. "Sit!" he ordered. "I get you coffee!"

Faye stepped back, grabbing onto Zantar's arm. "Efin, I have a new friend who is going to join me for coffee today. Efin," she said, then looked up, "this is Zantar. Zantar," she smiled over at the shorter man, "this is Efin, one of the best providers of coffee in the world!"

She laughed at the grunting sound coming from Zantar, hugging his arm before pulling away again. "Can you make that two cups of coffee?"

Efin nodded, then his eyes narrowed on Zantar's features. A moment later, he seemed more nervous, but Faye couldn't understand why.

"Yes!" he gasped, stepping backwards. "Yes, of course." The man seemed to bow, but since he just about tripped over the chair behind him, the bow wasn't very effective.

As soon as Efin had disappeared into the coffee shop to get their order, Faye turned to look up at Zantar. "What was that about?" she asked with a laugh, then shook her head as she dismissed the waiter's less than graceful departure. "We can sit over here. As much as I love the sunshine, the morning is getting warmer and I've discovered that this table's umbrella shields me from the sun better than the others."

He walked over and pulled out the metal chair for her. Faye was startled, not sure how to handle a man pulling a chair out for her. "Oh!" she gasped, stepping back slightly. After a brief hesitation, she sat down, feeling odd for a moment while she waited for Zantar to take the chair opposite her. Forgetting about Efin's odd behavior, she leaned forward, clapping her hands. "Okay, so tell me all about yourself! I'm dying to know how a man as big and tall as you are can stand wearing a suit in this kind of heat."

Faye stared into the man's dark eyes, fascinated.

"You're an interesting woman."

She laughed, waving his comment away with a sweep of her hand as she leaned back against the chair. "I'm nothing special," she replied. "But you," she countered, her eyes moving over his shoulders. "You're a linebacker, right?"

He laughed, shaking his head. "Close enough. What are you doing here in Skyla?"

Her grin widened. "I'm an art teacher back in Georgia. I teach high school art classes now," she started off. "I'm actually working on my PhD at the University of Georgia. I'm eager to move to the college level." She shrugged slightly. "I want to teach students who are more interested in art than what they anticipate to be an easy A." Her smile faded. "I'm here in Skyla working on my thesis."

"What is your topic?" he asked, but before Faye could reply, Efin arrived with a tray filled with two cups of coffee, cream, sugar, sweetener and a platter of pastries. He set everything onto the table, then bowed uncertainly, stepping backwards. "Compliments of the manager," he stated, stepping nervously to the side before he turned and hurried back into the coffee shop.

Faye stared at the now-closed door, confused. "Well, that was odd," she said as she turned back around. "Efin knows that I don't eat pastries."

She lifted her cup of coffee to her lips, taking a long sip. "Oh, this is so good!" she sighed. "We don't get coffee like this back in Georgia! I'm going to miss this when I'm finished here."

One dark eyebrow lifted in question as he took a sip of his own coffee. "You are going back to Georgia after you finish your research?"

"Yes," she explained, twisting her cup slightly. "I'm writing my thesis with funding from a federal grant during the kids' summer break, but working over at one of the big hotels to pay my extra living expenses. My research grant wasn't large enough to pay for everything during this period."

One dark eyebrow lifted with that explanation. "You are working two jobs?" he asked, his tone revealing his surprise.

"Oh, yeah," she laughed. "There's no way I could afford to live here while working on my thesis without a small bit of extra income. It's too expensive. Unfortunately, school teachers don't make very much money."

There was a slight narrowing of his eyes and Faye remained still under his perusal, allowing him to mentally work through whatever was going on inside that head of his.

"You were going to tell me about the subject of your doctoral research." He lifted one of the pastries and took a bite before placing the remainder back on the napkin.

Ah! A subject she could discuss with enthusiasm!

"I'm studying the symbols in the art of Agari Tismona," she explained, her eyes lighting with excitement. "There have been others who have studied similar symbols used by the Renaissance masters. These artists were revolutionaries and their artwork brought to light political intrigues to the masses." She leaned forward even more, her hands fluttering excitedly on the table. "The artists here in Skyla, like Tismona, probably had very little knowledge of the works being done by the Renaissance masters. And yet, their efforts were similar. Isn't it fascinating that art and architecture developed in separate parts of the world, but at the same rapid rate? And with the same style?"

"The style of architecture is different in the various parts of the world."

She nodded, then her butt wiggled as she eagerly explained. "Yes, I know that the architecture is different here compared to what we see in England or Ireland. But think about the magnificent churches of

England and compare them to the churches in Germany or France. The styles are shockingly similar. How is that possible? People didn't travel as much in that time period. So how did similar building practices evolve without..." she stopped, tilting her head slightly as she considered something. "I guess that the architects traveled and they knew of the old styles of building. But in art, it isn't like that. I mean, Tismona...he never traveled to Europe. And yet, his style of painting is similar, not exactly the same, but similar to many of the Renaissance masters, and there's so much symbolism in his work! How do all of the incongruous objects in his art tie together? What was his underlying message? What were his secret messages? Who were the secret messages meant for? Why didn't he just send a letter?"

Zantar watched the animation flit across her lovely features. Faye. What a beautiful name. Like a fairy, he thought. And that image wasn't too far from the truth. He could easily imagine the beautiful woman flitting away like an extraordinary Tinkerbell. The image caused his eyes to move lower, wondering what Faye would look like in the tiny green strapless dress that Tinkerbell normally wore. His mind remembered the skin tight material that Faye had on underneath the loose top and skirt. Yes, she'd look lovely in a tight, strapless dress. But not short. No, *his* Tinkerbelle wouldn't wear something short. She was too elegant for that. She'd wear...something long and drapey. A dress that floated out around her legs. But not too long. Her calves would show. And the dress would shimmer around her. Not green either. Blue. Yes, a blue dress that would match her shimmering, blue eyes.

"Zantar?"

He blinked, lifting his eyes back up to her features. "I apologize, *eazizi*." He took a sip of his coffee, hoping to hide the lust he was feeling at the moment. She was a startling beauty and the longer he listened to her speak, the more he wanted her.

"Are you okay?" she asked, reaching out to cover his hand with hers.

He looked down at their hands and concern hit him. Her hands were small with long, slender fingers. But those fingers...her nails were chipped and ragged, the skin around the cuticles rough and red. Some of her fingers had angry sores from blisters that had broken and were barely healing.

He started to turn his hand over so that he could examine her hand, and the wounds, more closely.

"Oh!" she gasped, trying to snatch her hand away in a futile effort to hide her hands from his penetrating gaze. But his reactions were swift and he caught her hands before she could hide them from his eyes.

"What happened to your hands?" he demanded, setting the ceramic cup down on the saucer as he turned her hands, examining the palms as well. There were more blisters, scrapes and sores on her palm and there was a redness creeping up along the pale skin of her forearm. "*Aljahim almuqadas!*" Zantar snarled, leaning forward to gently grasp her other hand, pulling it forward for his perusal. "How did this happen?"

She tugged at her hands, but he held her wrists firmly, careful not to hurt her wounds further, but unwilling to allow her to hide her blistered skin from his gaze. His stomach clenched and the lust was replaced by an instinctive need to protect.

"It's nothing," she whispered and he looked up at her, noting the way she bit her lower lip and her long, dark lashes lowered, as if she were trying to hide her pain or embarrassment.

"It's not nothing," he argued. "Answer me, *alsaghir*," he urged softly, but with a firm command.

"Zantar, it's nothing," she told him and twisted her hands. He couldn't hold onto the wrists without further damaging her skin when she moved in that way, so he released her hands and leaned back in his chair.

"Explain."

She laughed! The impertinent beauty actually laughed at him. Then she did something even more outrageous. She shook her head, denying him the knowledge that he'd requested!

"Let's talk about you. I've droned on and on about my research and my life. Will you please tell me something about yourself?" she asked, changing the subject with an engaging smile.

His eyes narrowed on her features, stunned that he'd given her a direct order and she'd...the woman had actually denied him! Did she not know who he was? The thought sent a small stab of hope throughout his body, pinging somewhere in his chest.

Ignoring the sensation, since he didn't fully understand it, he focused on her eyes. "What's on your agenda today?" he asked, thinking to find out the information he wanted in a different way.

Instantly, Faye brightened, her whole body coming alive once again. Her defensive posture disappeared as she leaned forward, gripping her coffee cup lightly with her hands a she smiled at him across the table. "This morning, I'll resume my examination of the paintings of Tismona. It's going to be fascinating since the museum director found several more examples of Tismona's paintings in storage! I'll get to examine paintings that have rarely been seen by the public! Hopefully, I can use those paintings to find a pattern in the symbolism that might reveal the secrets behind those symbols. So far, I've come up with several theories, but they are just theories right now. I don't have any concrete research to substantiate my ideas yet."

"Are you looking for proof?"

She shook her head and Zantar noticed that the sunshine now peeking over the buildings caused her hair to shine.

"No. Unfortunately, art historians can only make assumptions about an artist's intentions. It's very rare that we have actual proof of their thoughts. Sometimes, an artist writes letters to his or her family or friends. Those letters give us more insight into their intentions. But there are some artists, mine specifically, who didn't often write letters."

"I thought that letter writing was their main form of communication during that period?"

"It was," she smiled, shrugging slightly. "But not everyone was literate. And so far, I haven't been able to find many letters from this particular artist. There are some communications between the artist and his patrons, the people who hired him to paint for their families. But I have a sneaking suspicion that this artist was illiterate."

"Why do you think that?"

"Well, because his signature at the bottom of his paintings isn't anything like the letters that were written in his name. The initials are almost illegible, while the letters that were sent in his name are written clear, almost feminine in their wording and style."

"That sounds contradictory," he replied. "I see your conundrum."

She smiled briefly, but her eyes were intense now, revealing her intelligence and focus on the subject. "It's a fabulous mystery, but I hate not knowing a secret. I need to understand and have solid proof to back up my theories."

"How are you going to resolve your thesis then?"

She sighed, looking out at the now-busy streets. "I don't know yet." She glanced down at her watch and gasped. "I'm sorry," she said, standing up and grabbing her bulging cotton satchel. "I have to go or I'm going to be late."

Zantar stood as well, startled by the abrupt end of their discussion. Normally, he was the one to end meetings and it was shocking to be on the receiving end of the abruptness.

"You will meet me tomorrow for coffee again," he said, catching her hand and lifting it to his lips as he watched her eyes. He avoided hurting her wounds as he kissed the back of her hand.

"I will?" she asked, teasing him with a smile. But the woman moved closer. "I suppose that's possible."

"Faye," he growled, irritated that she hadn't instantly bowed to his authority. Granted, she didn't know about his authority, which was one of the reasons she intrigued him. He could see the desire reflected in her eyes and wanted to pull her into his arms. But something about her, perhaps the flare of anxiety in her eyes, prompted him to hold off. The lovely Faye was interested, but he also made her nervous. He'd have to work on easing her anxiety before he could kiss her, he thought.

"I really have to go," she whispered. "But yes, I will meet you here tomorrow for coffee again."

"I look forward to tomorrow," he replied, his voice lower than he'd anticipated, but there was just something about this woman that intrigued him, called to him.

Faye's soft lips opened slightly, and he noticed her irises dilate before she said, "Me too!"

With that, she stepped back and dug into her cotton bag. A moment later, she pulled out a handful of coins, dumping them onto the table. He glanced at the money and calculated that it was more than twice what the coffee and pastries should cost.

"I gotta go!" she called out, hurrying down the sidewalk.

Zantar turned to call out to her, intending to pick up the money she'd dumped and tell her to take most of it back. By the looks of her clothing and the fact that she wasn't driving anywhere, Zantar suspected that she wasn't wealthy. So why had she put down so much money?

Unfortunately, his thoughts scattered when she turned to look at him over her shoulder. The look in her eyes told him everything he needed to know. And it sealed her fate. The lovely Faye would be his. Soon!

Scott stared out at the large, seemingly barren landscape. But this… this was his chance! He could do this!

"You're a real prick."

Scott chuckled as Petro Zinhaden stood next to him. Both of them had sunglasses to protect their eyes from the intense sunshine. But that's where the similarities stopped. Scott was barely eight inches above five feet tall while Petro, a former KGB agent from Russia, was nearing six feet in height. Scott was soft where Petro was strong and powerfully built.

None of this bothered Scott though. He was the man who got promoted. During the last two efforts to extract the mineral efiasia from the earth, Scott had been everyone's lackey. But Harvey Neville, possibly the most despicable human being Scott had ever met, had passed over Petro for this third effort.

"Yeah, I might be a prick," Scott replied, "But I'm the prick that's in charge."

Petro snorted, the toothpick that he'd been chewing shifting to the opposite side of his mouth. "You're gonna fail." His smile was lethal. "And you'll end up just like the last two."

The scary man didn't wait for Scott's response. He simply turned and walked towards the line of dump trucks that were waiting for instructions. The massive drills would be put into place first, then the dump trucks would carry the useless sand, dirt and rocks away, putting it somewhere that wouldn't raise suspicions. Scott hadn't figured out where that dump site might be, but he had some ideas.

With a triumphant smile, he turned and headed towards the leader of the truck drivers. He had a job to do and he was going to get it done faster and better than his predecessors.

Chapter 2

"*Syid Latro*," she smiled in greeting to the museum's director as she stepped through the back entrance of the building. "It's wonderful to see you again!" she said in halting Arabic. She probably slaughtered the language, but she tried to learn new words every day and listened intently to others speak, hoping to improve her accent.

"*Yaftaqid Lafayette!*" the director greeted, using the formal and unmarried title instead of her first name, as she'd asked him to do repeatedly. But Mr. Latro, the museum director, was very old school and preferred the more formal way of speaking. Especially to unmarried women. Faye suspected that the more formal title created a barrier between them, reminding the man that she was unmarried and should be treated differently.

Unlike the daring Zantar, she thought. Even thinking his name sent a shiver of awareness throughout her body.

"You are cold," Mr. Latro replied, obviously sensing her shiver. "I will adjust the air conditioning for you."

The air conditioning in the building was set to "frigid", but Faye didn't want him to change it. "No, please don't," she urged as she followed the man through the hallways. "You're already doing so much to help me. I don't want to be a bother."

Mr. Latro waved aside her objections. "It is not a bother. And your work is very important. You are bringing attention to one of my favorite artists, a man who has been brutally neglected by the rest of the world. The renaissance 'masters'," he said, practically spitting with that last word, "should not be the only artists of that time period to be revered by the world. We have many artists that deserve accolades as well, and you will be the impetus that generates interest in our beautiful paintings."

Faye smiled, warmed by his words. "I'm honored that you think my doctoral dissertation will have that large of an impact."

"You are beautiful and young and enthusiastic. Your dissertation will bring this artists' work the recognition that he deserves, and the world will understand the beauty of *Syid* Tismona's work."

"I hope that you're right. He's a brilliant artist. I want people to recognize his genius." She sighed, shaking her head. "I just hope that I can figure it out and back up my theories."

Mr. Latro bowed slightly. "You will bring new heights of understanding to the symbolism in his works. I have faith in your abilities!"

Faye was warmed by his confidence. "Bring it on," she laughed. "Where are these paintings you were able to find in the storage areas?"

Mr. Latro waved her towards another section of the museum and Faye looked around at the tall shelves in a warehouse-like area. Here there were no smooth walls or discreet lighting which one would find in the tourist area of the museum. This was an industrial-looking room filled with wooden crates, cardboard boxes, and metal shelving that could hold tons of precious works of art off of the ground and out of danger. It was all categorized with computer generated bar codes and protected by armed guards walking through the aisles. Their steps echoed along the concrete floors as Mr. Latro led the way to a walled off room.

Faye had thought that he'd lead her to some type of conference room. But the door he pushed through was an elaborate, high-tech barrier that led to a space filled with the expensive equipment used to preserve old documents and care for precious paintings and other works of art.

Along the back wall, leaned up without frames, were ten new paintings, all of them appearing to be by her Tismona artist.

"Syid Latro!" Faye gasped, putting a hand to her chest as she surveyed the latest finds. "These are...beautiful!"

She moved quickly over to the paintings, her eyes scanning each image with reverence. "Magnificent!" she whispered when she'd reached the fifth one, but kept on walking, her feet not making a sound in this room. Obviously, vibrations were controlled in this area in order to protect artistic mediums that could crack or shatter in the wrong environment.

Mr. Latro agreed, but Faye was already absorbed in the content of the paintings, her eyes roaming over the canvases, taking in the details. Faye pulled her laptop out of her cotton bag, opening it up to start taking notes. Her cell phone was next as she took pictures of each new painting, changing the angles and shifting her focus to get more details so she could refer back to the pictures later.

"Set your alarm."

Faye looked up, startled by the man's words. "I'm sorry?"

Mr. Latro laughed softly, shaking his head. "You were late leaving here last week. Which I suspect meant that you were late getting to your next job?"

Faye groaned, remembering her mad rushes from the museum to the hotel to start her shift several days last week. Nodding her agreement, she clicked off of the camera app and pulled up her alarm. "Yes. You're right."

The director smiled beatifically at Faye, his hands clasped in front of him. "I thought so. You lose yourself in your work and that's a good thing. You will be happy for the rest of your life."

Faye smiled as she pressed several buttons. "Thank you for thinking of the alarm," she said, setting the time that would alert her to pack up in ninety minutes. She needed to get to the hotel in two hours in order start her shift on time today. Without her job at the hotel, she'd be seriously short of cash!

Her time doing research was only for another month, she told herself as she stuffed her phone back into her cotton bag, then pulled out a magnifying glass to continue her examination.

There was something different about these paintings. Faye bent lower, trying to figure out what that difference was. The colors were similar to the others by this artist that she'd studied. But…? All of the colors were the same. The image quality, brush strokes, signature and every other technical aspect of these paintings was similar. So they weren't done by a different artist.

So what was different?

She took several more pictures, focusing on the smaller details. In one painting, there was an apple held in a woman's hand, an odd looking chicken in the background of another, a glass of wine, a candle stick, an oil lamp, the edge of a window, the trees that seemed to be swaying in the breeze…everything was similar and yet…everything was different.

Carefully, Faye bent over, her magnifying glass in one hand while she wrote down thoughts with her other hand. Not notes so much as just scribbles, thoughts, impressions. She'd write all of these thoughts onto individual sticky notes and put each one up on the wall of her tiny apartment. Once everything was on the wall, she could move the sticky notes around, sort of like puzzle pieces that needed to be twisted and turned to find the right place to be added. Once she had a bigger picture, then she could hopefully make sense of these latest revelations.

She was just about to move on to the next painting when an alarm sounded. Faye jerked backwards, startled by the shrill sound in the silent room.

Glancing over at her phone, Faye stifled a frustrated snarl. She didn't want to go to the hotel today. She wanted to stay here and examine these paintings! She wanted to figure out what was different about these images!

And yet, they would still be here tomorrow, she thought. Yes, she would come back tomorrow for more research, spend more time with her mystery!

With a resentful sigh, Faye stuffed her laptop away and shoved her notebook and cell phone back into her bag. With a flip, she slung the cotton bag over her shoulder, patted her pockets to make sure she had her keys, then glanced at the time. Unfortunately, even with the alarm, she'd still have to hurry in order to reach her job at the hotel on time. Giving the paintings one last glance, she turned and headed out of the museum.

Chapter 3

"Faye?"

In the back of her mind, she heard someone call her name, but Faye ignored that niggling sound, preferring to think about the paintings, trying to pinpoint exactly what it was about them that was so different while she hurried down the sidewalk, ignoring the sun beating down on her head and shoulders. She went through her list of paintings in her mind, over and over again, staring at the sidewalk as she pondered the...!

"Faye!" a harsh, male voice snapped and, at the same time, someone grabbed her arm, pinching her skin with hard fingers.

Turning, she flung her heavy bag around, ready to tackle whoever had halted her momentum.

But as her eyes focused on the man standing in front of her, the anger cleared and a stunned shock slammed into her as she stared up at the smiling face. There was even a shiver of fear as she stared into the eyes of a man she'd thought to be firmly in her past.

Carefully, Faye backed away even as she forced her lips into a smile. "Scott!" she gasped, stepping backwards one more step. "What are you doing here, in Skyla?"

Scott Roland, her step-brother from back home, laughed, releasing her elbow and stretching his arms out wide. "Is that any way to greet your step-brother?" he asked.

Faye cringed and once again stepped backwards, needing more space between herself and this man. "We weren't ever very close," she said, crossing her arms over her chest as if to ward him off. She'd always felt a creepy, skeevy sensation whenever Scott was around. He was older than her by about five years, so by the time her mother had married Scott's father, Scott was already in college while Faye was finishing off her last two years of high school. But whenever Scott had come home for a visit, she'd always felt…icky. Scott had a way of looking at her that caused alarm bells to scream.

"I'm here on business," he replied, his eyes narrowing as he took in her defensive posture. "What about you?"

"Same," she replied, feeling lame even though it was the truth.

He snorted. "The little shits that take your high school art class need an understanding of Skyla's art world?"

Faye's whole body tightened at the sneering response. His demeanor was offensive and dismissive, insulting Faye and her life's work. Good grief, this man irritated her! He was even worse as an adult!

Shifting on her feet, she tried valiantly to smile politely. "I know that you're not a fan of art history, but I am. A lot of people find art soothing and interesting. Good art reveals truths in our souls that we weren't aware of."

He laughed again, shaking his head. "Whatever." He moved closer. "But since you're here, why don't I take you out for lunch?" he asked. His eyes shifted lower and Faye wished that she had a scarf or something to hide her body from his lecherous glances.

"I'm sorry, Scott, but I need to get to work." With that, she turned around and headed back towards the hotel, praying that he wouldn't follow her. Just to be kind, she turned and said over her shoulder, "It was nice running into you again. Good luck with your business!" She bit her lip at the obvious lie as she raced down the sidewalk, desperate to get away from the man.

The hotel locker room was busy when she stepped through the employee entrance but Faye smiled to several of her coworkers as she rushed over to her locker. Quickly, she changed into her uniform, grabbed the cleaning cart filled with all of the toxic cleaning supplies that had torn up her hands over the past several weeks, and pushed the heavy cart down the hallway along with the others on the cleaning team.

For the next eight hours, she cleaned mirrors, scrubbed toilets, sanitized showers, stripped and remade beds, fluffed pillows and cleared away the disgusting plates and dishes that the previous temporary tenants of each room had left on the hallway floor after devouring a late night snack from the room service menu. The plates were now crusted with dried food and surrounded by trash, but Faye picked everything up and cleaned until her back ached.

The rooms in this hotel were actually beautiful. The upscale grey and white décor was enhanced by tasteful art and lush green plants. But the biggest and best room was the penthouse. Faye hadn't ever seen that space, being the lowest on the seniority list for cleaning employees, but she'd heard about it. The two-story apartment was reputed to be lovely, with crystal chandeliers and wide, soft sofas, several bedrooms and even a small kitchen, although normally the food would be prepared in the hotel's main kitchen on the ground floor. That food would then be whisked up to the penthouse via a special food elevator and received in a butler's pantry manned by a genuine butler and served on fine china.

At the end of her shift, Faye rubbed medicated lotion onto her painfully sore hands, ignoring the sting as the cream sank into several new cuts and blisters. As she put her street clothes back on, Faye wondered what it would be like to spend just a few nights in the penthouse suite. She imagined it would be nice, having servants wait on her, prepare her meals and, even better, she'd never clean another toilet again!

"You okay?" one of the other housekeeping team members asked, slamming her locker closed as everyone slowly grabbed their personal items and moved towards the exit, heading to their homes. At this point in the day, no one moved very fast. The energy required to clean just one hotel room was shocking, and each of them had cleaned more than twenty that day.

"I'm fine," she sighed, knowing that it was a lie.

The woman looked at Faye's hands, then at her own roughness as well as scars from where her skin had cracked and blistered, then healed over. "You really should have those blisters looked at. They don't look good."

Faye spread her hands out wide, nodding her acknowledgement of the abuse. "I know. I think you're right." But she simply pushed her hands into the pockets of her skirt. "I'll do that on my next day off." It was another lie. She didn't have any health insurance here in Skyla, because the country's national health care was only for citizens. It was actually pretty good, but as a foreigner on a temporary visa, she didn't have a health card. So she'd have to pay out of pocket for any doctor's visit. Unfortunately, she didn't make enough money to risk a doctor's visit. Better to wait until she got home to Georgia where she could use her teaching job's health insurance.

Until then, she'd just make sure that her hands were clean and use lots of lotion.

Stepping out of the building through the employee entrance, Faye lifted her face up to the slowly fading sunshine, pushing the issue of her hands out of her mind for the moment. It was a beautiful night and Faye loved the warmth of this country, as well as the friendly people and exotic foods. Unfortunately, the aches in her back and feet from the day's work clamored for relief.

It was only five o'clock in the evening when she let herself into her tiny apartment, but she tumbled onto the small bed and slept the sleep of the dead, exhaustion hitting her harder than any time before.

Unfortunately, she didn't sleep very well. She had dreams of a tall, muscular man ordering her about. Faye shivered in her sleep as she disobeyed every order the man gave her, enjoying his growling "retribution" for her disobedience.

Chapter 4

Faye finished her yoga on the beach earlier than usual the next morning, too excited to see Zantar. Although, she had to acknowledge a bit of anxiety at the thought of seeing him again. After last night's dreams, and all the salacious things that he'd done to her in those dreams, she was more than a bit embarrassed to face the man.

Logically, her reaction didn't make much sense. There wasn't any way that he could know what had happened in her dreams. Good grief, she had no idea where the man lived, much less where he'd slept last night. And yet, she blushed every time she thought about her dreams. They had been so…real!

After stretching her muscles and doing her sun salutations, greeting the morning, and regaining her positivity after yesterday's brutal cleaning schedule, Faye hurried down the street, her legs eagerly stretching to reach the coffee shop. Was she being too eager? Probably, Faye told herself. And yet, she didn't slow down.

As soon as she stepped around the corner, she saw him! He was there! And yes, the impressive, glorious man was just as big and handsome and alluring and…sigh…amazing as she remembered from yesterday. His presence literally took her breath away and Faye stood still for a moment, admiring the man.

She'd realized this morning that he hadn't revealed anything about himself during their time together yesterday. He had deftly turned her questions back to her. So today, Faye was determined to ask him more. She was going to discover something real about this man. Something personal.

"Good morning," she gushed as he stood up at her approach. He tossed the newspaper he'd been reading onto the table, looking down at her. He wasn't smiling, but for some reason, she knew that he was pleased to see her. Perhaps it was in his eyes? She didn't know. Nor did she understand why this man affected her so dramatically. None of the men she'd dated in the past had really sparked any interest in her over the years. They'd all been nice and friendly. But Zantar...he sparked an inferno!

"*Sabah alkhayr*, Faye," he greeted, taking her hands and lifting them to his lips. With a softness that belied the muscles on his tall body, he kissed her fingertips lightly and more of those delicious shivers raced through her body. "You look lovely. Did you greet the day on the beach again this morning?"

Faye's lungs felt as if they had been deprived of air as she stared up at the man. He was just so tall and...and male! Never before had she felt this strong of an attraction to another man in her life.

"*Sabah alkayr*, Zantar," she whispered back to him. "And yes, I did my morning sun salutations on the beach this morning."

For a long moment, the rest of the world faded away. It was just herself and this man. There was no bustling traffic or other commuters walking along the sidewalk. It was simply this man and the intense awareness that rolled through her body.

"Did you have breakfast?" he asked, moving closer.

Breakfast? Had she eaten this morning? "Yes!" she gasped. "Oh, erm, yes! I had breakfast already. But the coffee...I always stop here for coffee after..." she waved her hand in the general direction of the beach. "After I exercise."

He took her hand and led her to the chair next to where he'd been sitting moments ago. "How was your investigation yesterday? Did you discover anything new about your artist?" When they were seated, he poured her a cup of coffee, then nudged the cream and sugar closer to her.

Zantar watched as Faye lifted the cup to her lips, savoring the rich, fragrant brew. She closed her eyes and tilted her head ever so slightly. It was an erotic expression and he wondered what she'd look like once he pleasured her. He wanted to put that look of bliss on her lovely features. He wanted to give her pleasure and hear her sighs of contentment.

Shifting in his chair, he wondered what the other patrons would do if he lifted her over the table and settled her on his lap so he could feel her pleasure as well as see it.

Soon, he told himself. Soon, he would have this woman in his bed. Normally, he'd never take this much time to court a woman. If she was willing upon their first meeting, and he was interested, then he'd give the woman pleasure before finding his own. He'd kept mistresses over the years, but when those relationships had ended, he hadn't been overly concerned.

Seeing Faye now, he knew that his relationship with her wouldn't be superficial like the others. No, there was something special about her. He'd cursed Sheik Astir del Taran and Goran al Istara when he'd heard what was potentially going on along their shared border. He hadn't wanted to come here and listen to the problems of the other two leaders. But now that he was once again sitting across from Faye, he would have to give both men credit. If this crisis hadn't come about, he never would have met Faye. And she was definitely worth the trip.

But he was startled when she shook her head. "No, I'm not going to answer any more questions until you tell me more about yourself." She stared over the rim of her coffee cup at him. "I left here yesterday knowing your name and..." her eyes drifted over his body, "and that you have yummy shoulders. Nothing else."

He forgave her impudence simply because she called his shoulders "yummy". His guards were sitting at the other tables and one of them snorted. Later, he'd discover the name of the man and would use him for practice on the mat. But for the moment, he wanted to discover more about Faye. She fascinated him and he didn't like her holding back any information about herself.

"I practice judo and tai kwon do every day," he said, wondering if his guards had taken the hint.

Faye's eyes widened. "That's interesting! I've often thought about taking a self-defense class but I keep putting it off because..." she tilted her head from side to side. "Well, because I'm a bit intimidated and I don't really want to learn. It's just something that I feel as if I *should* learn." She leaned her elbows on the table. "So why do you?'

"Why do I what?"

"Why do you practice self-defense?" she clarified. Her eyes drifted over his shoulders once again before coming back to look him in the eye.

He shrugged. "I enjoy the physical exertion," he replied, even if that was only half the truth. "What did you learn about your artist yesterday?"

She shook her head again, her grin widening as her eyes sparkled with challenge. "Nope. I want more." One dark eyebrow lifted, but she merely laughed at his expression. "Don't even try it, Zantar," she chided. "I know your name, that you're hot, and that you know a few self-defense moves." She grinned. "How old are you?"

Zantar leaned back in his chair, amused and…surprisingly, he enjoyed her daring. "I'm thirty-five," he replied succinctly.

"What's your favorite color?"

"I don't have one."

Her own brown eyebrow lifted at that. "What color is your bedroom?"

He stared at her for a long moment, then he blinked and she realized that he didn't know. At least, not off the top of his head.

"Brown," he guessed.

Her lips pulled into a grimace. "What a tedious color, Zantar!'

He almost laughed at her response. Almost! In the end, he maintained his stoic expression. "What color is your bedroom?"

Faye tilted her head slightly and he noticed several different colors within the soft brown tresses. A few were golden and some were darker. Fascinating, he thought.

"Well, the bedroom in which I'm staying at the moment has tan walls and a tan comforter with white sheets and brown carpeting that I don't think has been cleaned since the nineteen seventies."

Faye almost laughed at his stern expression. "Why are you staying in such a hovel?" he demanded and she discerned from the tension now in those amazing shoulders that he was angry with her.

"Because it's cheap," she replied, wanting to soothe his anger, but not sure how. "It's really not that bad, Zantar. I don't spend a great deal of time in that place. I'm either at the museum reviewing the pictures, or I'm ensconced in Skyla's impressive library researching historical documents and books on my artist's life or," she cringed and hid her hands under the table, "I'm working at the hotel."

"Why are you working at a hotel?"

Faye leaned back in her chair, enjoying the warmth of the sunshine as well as the heat from his eyes. Goodness, she felt beautiful sitting across from him!

"Because I need the money. We discussed this yesterday."

"And yet, you gave the waiter an outrageous tip yesterday. Obviously, you need the money more."

"No," she shook her head. "Efin has two kids and works three jobs in order to support them. His wife died two years ago and his mother takes care of his kids while he's working." Faye wasn't aware of her eyes turning sad. "It would break my heart if I had a child and I didn't see them in the morning and evening."

"You would stay home after giving birth," he stated firmly.

Faye considered his comment, taking it as a question instead of a statement, then shook her head. "No, I don't think I could do that. My limited salary as a teacher and even, hopefully, as a professor, would mean that I'd have to continue to work. My current salary wouldn't cover my living expenses for a long-term absence."

His only response was a grunt and Faye smiled. "I take it that you would remain at home with your children?"

The surprise on his ruggedly handsome features was comical. "My wife will raise our children!"

"Why do you assume that?" she asked, tilting her head to the side. This man definitely needed an education on equality!

Zantar stared at Faye for a long moment, trying to determine if she was teasing him again. He didn't think so. After waking up this morning with a painful erection caused by intensely erotic dreams featuring this woman, he'd decided that Faye would be the mother of his children. To that effect, he'd had his security team do a quick background check on her and she appeared to be everything she'd told him yesterday. She was employed as a high school art teacher with outstanding performance reviews, and her doctoral dissertation had been mostly funded by grants provided by the National Endowment for the Arts. By all accounts, she was a hardworking, dedicated teacher.

And the woman had a figure that he wanted to possess! Although, at the moment, he wanted to drag her across his lap and spank her adorable bottom!

"What is your favorite color?" he demanded, changing the subject. He wasn't going to argue about women caring for the children. If she didn't want to stay home and care for their children, he knew that she would be a caring mother in other ways. Besides, he wanted to be an active father in his children's lives as well.

The woman's smile was slow and sexy, causing his stomach to tighten as he tried to control his reaction to her beauty and her...yes, he was even attracted to her daring. He admitted that he was more than slightly sexist. But he could learn, he told himself. Perhaps Faye could teach him to be more aware of women and their issues, concerns, and needs.

"You're diverting the conversation away from yourself again. How about this," she offered, cradling her coffee in her hands. "Let's play twenty questions. I ask you simple questions and you answer them."

"Just twenty?" he teased, amused by her game.

She gave him a gamine smile and lifted one shoulder. "Okay, maybe more than twenty."

Zantar leaned forward, lightly clasping his hands in front of him. "I will agree to this line of questioning as long as you answer the questions as well."

Faye considered his offer, then nodded. "Fine." She lifted a finger, tapping it against her chin. "Okay, so I know that you're thirty-five and you prefer the color brown." She considered her first question carefully. "What's your favorite food?"

"I will try anything," he replied. "And yours?"

She shook her head. "Nope. You didn't answer the question. I'm sure that you're manly enough to try anything someone sets in front of you." Her head tilted slightly. "You probably have to endure numerous business dinners in which you are required to politely eat whatever is served."

"This is true," he agreed, although he wouldn't call them business dinners per se. They were political or diplomatic events, and he hated each and every one of them. If he had his way, he'd delegate all of those events to his diplomats or agency heads. Unfortunately, that wasn't always possible.

"I didn't ask you to name a food that you won't eat. I asked what your favorite food is." She shifted on her chair, revealing both her eagerness and a tempting shadow between her breasts through the floaty blouse she'd donned earlier today. But in Zantar's mind, he pictured the tight, mesh exercise material she'd worn yesterday morning.

"Sweet potatoes." He blurted out. It was the first thing that came to mind and he blinked, lifting his surprised eyes back to hers. "I like sweet potatoes." He shifted in his chair. "As a child, I remember my mother's excitement over fried sweet potatoes." His mouth twisted briefly before he continued. "I don't like the kind of sweet potato casseroles that are covered in marshmallows or other sweet stuff."

"That's interesting. What did your mother put on your sweet potato fries?"

Zantar doubted that his mother ever knew where the kitchen was within the palace, so she'd never actually cooked anything. "They were spicy, but I don't remember what kinds of spice was used. And there was a sour cream and salsa kind of dipping sauce that was always served with the fries." He nodded firmly. "So in answer, spicy sweet potato fries."

Faye blinked and his mind wandered back to sex. Actually, had it ever really left sex? Not when Faye was around. Or not around, he thought as he considered his dreams the previous night. He was pretty impressed with how much he'd just revealed to her with that explanation about his favorite food.

"I like sweet potatoes too," she replied, and a slight blush swept over her tanned skin. It looked lovely, he thought. A blush. How long had it been since he'd seen a woman blush? Ever?

"But that tuber isn't your favorite food, is it?" he asked, seeing something strange in her eyes. He didn't understand that look. Not yet. But Zantar was determined to figure this woman out. Her allure had now gone beyond the superficial. He wanted more than to just know her body. He wanted to understand her.

"Potato chips," she whispered, her lips curling into a slow grin that told him that potato chips weren't just her favorite food, it was her decadent sin! Zantar was unaware of his own secret smile.

"What kind of car do you drive?"

He almost laughed at that. "I am generally in a black SUV." Then he lifted his eyebrow, waiting for her answer.

"I drive a very sensible Toyota Prius. It gets excellent gas mileage!" she replied proudly.

He chuckled as her adorable expression shifted slightly. "That's a good car," he replied. "What color?"

"Black," she sighed. "The Prius gets excellent gas mileage, but it isn't sporty. I thought that the black color would make it look sexier. Maybe even encourage it to be a tough little bully while driving to work every day." Her lips twisted, then she laughed. "It didn't. The little guy is good, but he's not going to outrace the BMWs on the road pushing all of the other cars around."

He almost laughed at her description. "You would prefer to drive a BMW?"

Once again, Faye laughed, shaking her head and causing her hair to shimmer in the overhead sunlight. "No. Not a BMW."

"What is your favorite vehicle?" he asked, thinking he could order one and have it delivered.

Unfortunately, Faye simply shook her head. "I'm not really into cars. All that's important to me is fuel-efficiency. Save the environment and all that."

Zantar grunted, wondering if she was telling him the truth.

But before he could question her further, she asked the next question. "Tell me the strangest thing that's on your bucket list."

Zantar stared at her with confusion. "What is a bucket list?"

Her mouth fell open. "You don't have a bucket list?" When he merely lifted an eyebrow, she continued. "It's just a list of things that you want to do before you die. Some people put sky diving or traveling to various countries, learning a foreign language...things like that."

He didn't have a bucket list. Since he'd already been to almost every country in the world, or at least the ones that he wanted to visit, plus several that he'd be very happy to never see again, that possibility was knocked off the list. He also spoke several languages fluently, rode horses better than most, had gone through military training that had led him through both jungles and deserts as well as other insane environments. He knew how to jump out of planes, could even fly the plane as well as helicopters and…hell, he had no idea what he wanted on his personal list of things-to-do. Then he realized exactly what he wanted.

"I want to find a woman to marry and have a large family," he stated succinctly, thinking that having children, specifically with Faye, would be a pivotal moment in his life. As soon as he had the thought, he knew that he wanted that more than anything else in the world.

Her smile faltered slightly, although Zantar had no idea why. But she merely said, "That's a very nice goal." She glanced at her cell phone and sighed. "I'd better get to the museum."

He stood as well, then stalled her hand when she reached into her cotton bag to pull out money. "I will pay for the coffee this morning," he assured her. "Will you have time tomorrow to show me your work at the museum?"

Her hand pulled out of her bag, but he could see the indecision in her eyes. He wanted to warn her that she needed to get used to him paying. After yesterday's surprise handful of coins, he knew that he'd never allow her to pay for anything with him again. Hell, he wanted to tell her to move out of her rental space, quit her job and he'd find an apartment for her! Even better, he wanted to claim her, bring her back to his private quarters within the Citran palace and make love to her until she finally agreed to marry him so that he could make every one of her personal bucket list items a reality.

But he doubted Faye would allow that. She seemed like a very independent sort of woman and putting her up in an apartment reeked of "mistress". Even he didn't like what that implied.

"You want to see the paintings I'm studying?" she asked, her voice hesitantly excited.

"I would sincerely enjoy discovering anything that puts that excitement on your features," he told her.

"Oh!" she grinned, shifting, then looking to the right then the left before looking at him again. She cleared her throat, staring at his chest. "I would be honored to show you my work. But I'll have to check with the museum director. *Syid* Latro is a very capable director, but he's also careful about who he allows into the museum. I don't want to impose on his generosity by bringing a stranger into his museum. Especially since he's allowed me access to the back areas where there isn't as much security."

"Give me the name of the museum and I'll speak with *Syid* Latro to assure him of my altruistic intentions." He actually didn't have an altruistic bone in his body when it came to Faye. No, his intentions were much more…basic. Carnal, even. And yet, he also wanted to ensure that she was safe. It was a very odd sensation, he thought. One he wasn't used to, but he liked the idea of protecting Faye from the harsh world.

"No!" she gasped, shaking her head again. "That's okay. I'll speak with him today as soon as I arrive. No need to bother yourself when I'll see him in a few minutes."

He moved closer, not liking the nervousness that had entered her voice. "Which museum, Faye?" he asked, his voice lowering in an effort to convey his authority.

Unfortunately, he'd forgotten that Faye ignored his authority. Her light laughter stunned him, but not nearly as much as the touch of her hand on his chest. He was so surprised by her soft fingers, even through the layers of his suit, vest, and shirt, he couldn't speak for a long moment.

"Don't be silly," she told him, pulling her hand away. "Will I see you tomorrow?"

"Yes," he growled, wanting to say something more, but before he could get the words out, she had already skipped away.

"I look forward to tomorrow then!" she called and almost danced down the sidewalk away from him! Damn her, she had no idea who he was!

Then he realized what had just passed through his mind. She had no idea who he was. She was interested in him. Not his title or his power. Just him!

The surge of lust that thought engendered inside of him caused him to almost smile. Almost! She'd still disobeyed him! He'd definitely have to remove that inclination from her personality, he told himself as he moved to the line of SUVs that pulled up moments later.

But even as he pulled the door closed, he stopped his thoughts. He didn't want Faye to be like all of the other women who had traipsed through his life. He loved her free spirit and the way she trampled over his authority. No, he wasn't going to get rid of that inclination. But it was time to step up his plan so that he could stop her disobedience in a much more delightful manner.

Chapter 5

Faye was almost humming as she left the museum that morning, heading down the street towards the hotel. No, she didn't want to work this afternoon. But she needed the money. She'd get paid in a few days but, until that money hit her account, she'd be living off of peanut butter and cheap bread. Her financial situation wouldn't be so dire if she hadn't needed to purchase a new laptop. Her trusty old laptop had died last week, and it had been imperative that she purchase a new one. Back in Georgia, she knew a guy who sold refurbished laptops and would sell one to her for less than he charged other customers, simply because his daughter had been a student in her classroom a few years ago. But here in Minar, the capital city of Skyla? She wasn't sure where to purchase a used laptop, much less someone trustworthy who would have refurbished the computer properly. So she'd bought a new, inexpensive laptop that wasn't very fast, but it got the job done.

Unfortunately, that also meant that money was pretty tight now. She'd get through the next few days until payday though.

Still, she wasn't going to allow her financial stress to ruin a perfectly beautiful day! Lifting her face up to the sunshine, she smiled as the warmth revived her. It was hard being inside the cold museum for the first few hours of the day. There were no windows and, as usual, Mr. Latro preferred the air conditioner to be set at frigid temperatures! Why did he want the space so cold? She'd learned to bring a sweater for those few hours that she lost herself in the paintings.

Thankfully, she was out of the frigid air. Regretfully, she still had a shift at the hotel in which she needed to work.

Sighing, she trudged down the sidewalk, not as energetically as earlier, but still determined. While she waited to get paid, maybe she could sneak something to eat from the hotel kitchens. If there was food left over from an event, the staff were generally permitted, even encouraged, to eat the leftovers.

"Hi everyone!" she called out as she stepped through the employee entrance. How many more days until her days off? Too many, she thought as she worked her way towards her locker. Quickly, Faye pulled on her uniform, stuffed the rest of her belongings into the locker and shut everything away before making her way to the cleaning carts. She did a fast inventory, accepted her room assignments then...!

"Wait!" she called out to her boss. Pointing at the assignment sheet, she looked at Tamas. "Why am I in the penthouse today?"

Tamas shrugged and looked down at his clipboard. "Asila is out sick today, and you've done a great job in the other rooms. I'm promoting you." He looked at her over his thick glasses. "Just for today. Don't get used to it!"

Faye laughed, delighted with the easier schedule. "Great!" she told her boss, then did a little jig as she walked out of the locker rooms.

Ten minutes later, she pushed her cart through the special doors to the penthouse suite. She didn't use the main doors. Those were exclusively for the guests. Nope, she and the other hotel staff were required to use the less auspicious staff doors. They were scratched and dented, very lackluster. The maintenance personnel didn't fix these issues because there wasn't any reason to impress the hotel staff.

"You're new!" a man in a dark suit snapped. His dark eyes moved up and down over her figure. "I heard that Asila is sick today. Are you up to the task of cleaning the penthouse?"

Faye swallowed the sharp, angry retort. She was just a cleaning team member here, she reminded herself. She wasn't a teacher here and there was definitely a hierarchy of staff members in the hotel. Cleaning team members were absolutely the lowest on that hierarchy!

"Just tell me where you need me to start, and I'll be fast and thorough." She realized that was the right thing to say when the butler nodded sharply.

"Start in the master suite. It's on the second floor, all the way to the end. You'll see the double doors at the end of the hallway."

Faye nodded and pushed her cart towards the staff elevator. Moments later, she pushed her cart out into what was possibly the most beautiful room she'd ever seen. It was done all in shades of white and shimmering silver. It was somehow both extravagant and practical, with thick throw blankets on the end of the bed as well as over chairs that looked to be deep and comfortable. A body could curl up in one of those chairs and never need to get up, she thought with a wishful sigh.

The bathroom was just as heavenly, with a massive bathtub that would comfortably fit six or seven people. It was deep, like a small pool, and framed by a large window that looked out over the capital city. From this high up, there wasn't any possibility of people looking in on the bathers, but still, the concept was quite decadent. There was white marble everywhere, with black trim and faucets. The whole effort was stark and lovely.

"Not here to admire everything," she whispered to herself and pulled out the cleaning supplies. She'd grabbed a pair of rubber gloves from the kitchen yesterday and the barrier between her hands and the cleaning supplies had helped significantly. Thankfully, this pair of gloves hadn't melted yet. Just having one day without the harsh chemicals on her skin had helped some of the blisters heal up. Keeping that in mind, she was careful when she scrubbed the white marble today, not wanting to lose that barrier by scraping the rubber on anything that might tear it and allow the chemicals to touch her skin.

She'd just finished the bathroom when she heard talking. At first, she'd assumed that it was that uppity butler coming to snap at her, tell her that she wasn't cleaning thoroughly enough or that she was taking too long. Carefully, Faye stuffed her rubber gloves into the pockets of her cleaning uniform, then hurriedly pushed the cleaning cart out of the bathroom and into the bedroom. Faye had done an excellent job in there!

"Faye?" a harsh, raspy masculine voice demanded.

Faye lifted her head sharply, her eyes widening as she took in the tall, powerful form of Zantar as he stood in the middle of the bedroom.

"Zantar?" she whispered, her lips going numb as she took in his tall form, minus the jacket and vest he'd had on only hours before. Underneath the crisp, tailored dress shirt, she could discern the lean waist and flat stomach as well as his long, powerful legs. She realized that she'd never seen his legs before because they'd been sitting at the table or she'd been too overwhelmed by his presence to notice anything other than his rugged features. His dark, forbidding eyes had always made her anticipate trying to make the man smile.

"This is where you work?" he demanded, moving closer to her.

Startled by his approach, she stepped back, but the cleaning cart was behind her and she was trapped. "Um…yes. But…I'm not here trying to stalk you! I promise! I was only assigned to the penthouse suite for today's shift. There's no way I could have known I'd be here, and you can ask my boss. He'll tell you that he assigned me to this area himself. I didn't urge him to assign me here."

He put a finger to her lips and Faye had the insane urge to stick out her tongue, to taste that finger. It was tempting. The man was tempting! He was big and tall and powerful! And the bed! Oh, good grief, the bed was so close!

Faye had to remind herself that she wasn't the kind of woman who slept with men on a casual basis. Good grief, she wasn't even the kind of woman to sleep with a man on a formal basis! So this...everything here was completely out of her realm of experience.

"I know, Faye," he replied gently. Unfortunately, his voice was the only part of him that was soothing! The rest of his body, big and muscular, was too close. She could smell him! And boy, did he smell good! A little spicy, a bit of the woods in the background and all male. Definitely male!

His hand slid around, cupping the back of her head. "I didn't make the connection that you worked in the same hotel in which I am staying." He paused, his eyes lighting with mischief even as the rest of his features remained stern and uncompromising. "You might assume that I've orchestrated your presence here in order to seduce you."

Her heart pounded at the idea. "Did you?" she whispered, her voice betraying her hope at the possibility. She quickly cleared her throat. "No! Of course you didn't manipulate the cleaning teams' schedule and have me sent up here. That's silly." She stepped back, or tried to, but the cleaning cart was still pressing against her back. She shook her head, trying to figure out what she was doing. Or what she should be doing. Surely there was some funny comment she could make that would ease the increasing tension rising between them.

"I will just...get out of your way," she told him.

"You don't have to hurry out of here," he replied, his voice even huskier than moments ago. "In fact, I think..." he stopped abruptly.

Faye had been staring at the middle of his chest, fascinated by what might be underneath the expensive material of his shirt when he stopped speaking. Instantly, she knew that he was distracted by something and lifted her gaze to find him reaching behind her. A moment later, he held one of the cleaning bottles aloft. "Is this what you and the others in the hotel use to clean the rooms?" he demanded.

His voice was no longer husky. Instead, he sounded furious for some reason. "Yes," she finally replied, glancing at the bottle of spray cleaner in his hands.

Speaking of hands, he lifted one of hers up, examining the blisters. They didn't look nearly as bad as the first day she'd met him, but the skin was still raw and covered with barely healed blisters.

"This contains phosphoric acid, Faye!" he growled, turning her hands over, examining all sides. "This is something that should be used to clean industrial equipment, and there should be more than just safety gloves between you and it. Hell, you should be wearing full body protective gear as well as a mask to prevent lung damage when using this stuff!"

Faye wasn't sure what to say. She hadn't ever argued about the chemicals that had been in her cart. Everyone's hands on the cleaning team looked rough, although most of the other team members were more used to the cleaning products and didn't have any actual blisters anymore. They all sported impressive scars though, so Faye understood that, at some point, their skin had been just as torn up as hers.

"This stuff is toxic, Faye!" he snapped and walked out of the bedroom, gently but firmly tugging her with him but being careful to keep his hands on her arm and not touching her hands any longer.

He marched into the kitchen, his features set in furious lines.

The man in the dark suit, who Faye assumed was the butler, instantly pushed away from the countertop where he'd been talking and laughing with another staff member. But at the sight of Zantar stepping into the butler's area, the man appeared horrified before he regained his composure.

"Is there something...?" he started, only to be interrupted by Zantar.

"Get the hotel manager up here now!" he snapped.

The butler blinked, startled by the furious command. But the man was a professional and recovered quickly. It took him perhaps two seconds before he bowed and replied, "Yes, your..."

"And I want the hotel doctor up here too. If there isn't a doctor on staff, then call someone immediately!" He lifted Faye's hands in the air, showing the butler the blisters and scratches, the raw, painful looking skin. "This is inexcusable! No one should be forced to endure this kind of pain simply because the hotel demands that the cleaning staff use toxic chemicals to clean the suites!"

The butler, normally so formal-looking and uppity, was stammering now.

Faye shrank back, sure that she was going to be fired over this little incident. Cleaning staff did not raise a ruckus about their duties. They clocked in, cleaned their assigned rooms, clocked out and did it all over again the next day.

"Zantar, this isn't necessary," she whispered, trying to convey with her eyes that he was out of line.

His own gaze shot down to her and she actually backed up at the fury in those dark depths. "It is very necessary!" he growled. He turned to look at the butler. "Where is the hotel manager? And a doctor?!"

The butler literally tripped on his feet as he stumbled backwards at that command. He rushed through the doors at the back of the pantry, obviously eager to be away from Zantar's wrath.

Faye jerked her arm away from Zantar. Poking him in the chest, she glared up at him. "If you get me fired from this job, Zantar, I swear I'm going to…!"

She stopped as she tried to come up with something truly vile to hold over his head.

He leaned forward, his eyes daring her. "You'll do what?" he asked, the anger gone from his voice which had turned soft and sexy once again. When she still hesitated, he lifted a dark eyebrow. "Please Faye, I'm eager to hear what sort of punishment you will impose on me for standing up for your rights, and the rights of every other staff member in this hotel, to not be tortured by an acid-based cleaning solution that shouldn't be near a human body." He leaned closer and she could smell his minty breath. "Ever!"

She swallowed, not sure where to go from there. He wasn't backing down. Her students always backed down when she started to issue threats. She could be quite intimidating when she needed to be. And being an art teacher, in a classroom filled with some students that truly didn't want to learn anything about art, she'd learned to be adept at keeping students on task.

"I'll do something horrible, Zantar! And I will be very angry!"

He laughed softly, his eyes boring into hers as he shook his head. "I'm not afraid of you, little one."

"I'm not little," she argued, then looked at his broad shoulders, acknowledging the fact that she was little compared to him. "You're just big!"

He chuckled. "You're very correct, Faye."

Their conversation was interrupted when the butler rushed back into the area, followed closely by the hotel manager.

Faye had only seen the hotel manager at a distance, but she knew that she didn't like the man. He was even more uppity than the butler and literally sneered at the members of the cleaning staff if he ever had to pass them in the hallways during his work hours.

"I understand that there is…." The manager started to say, only to be interrupted by Zantar as he lifted the bottle of cleaning solution in the air.

"Why is the cleaning staff using this to clean the hotel?" he demanded, his voice snarling now. "This is a toxic chemical and should only be used in industrial settings." He stopped, then turned and lifted Faye's hands. "This is what the chemical does to unprotected skin!"

The hotel manager's mouth was tight with fury, but when he looked over at Faye's hands, his jaw went slack with horror. "Dear heaven!" he whispered. "What happened to you?"

Faye tried to pull her hands away, and the hotel manager understood that she was not responsible for this complaint. He pulled himself upright, nodding to Zantar. "Quite right, Your…"

"And where is the doctor?" Zantar demanded, interrupting the manager once again. "I want a doctor to take a look at Faye's hands and then she or he needs to examine your entire hotel cleaning staff. I suspect that they might even have lung or liver damage caused by the toxic fumes." Zantar's eyes narrowed as he looked down at the man. "And I'm sure that the hotel will cover the medical costs for every person this doctor examines, correct?"

The hotel manager's mouth opened and closed. His eyes moved over to Faye and she swallowed, terrified that she was going to be fired as soon as Zantar went off to his next meeting.

"Of course!" the manager replied, bowing to Zantar. The guy actually bowed!

Faye glanced up at Zantar and mentally agreed with the guy. Zantar was a pretty intimidating man. However, before this moment, she'd always considered the engaging look in his eyes to be more alluring than the intimidation he tried to convey to the rest of the world.

Zantar barely glanced at her before looking towards the butler. The man immediately lifted his hands and nervously slipped away as well.

"Come," he ordered, tugging Faye out of the butler's area and into the big open space that might be called a "great room" in a house. Faye had no idea what it was called here in the penthouse. The hotel probably had some crazy name for the space, but Faye jerked her arm out of his grip, causing him to spin around to glare down at her.

"I need you to stop!" she hissed, glancing around to make sure that none of the other hotel staff were within earshot.

"Stop?" he growled. "You've been seriously harmed because of poor hotel management and you want me to stop?"

"You're going to get me fired!"

He moved so that he was standing a mere inch away from her and Faye couldn't stop the thought that she wished he'd take her into his arms and hold her. She was scared that she'd be fired as soon as she left this space. If she were fired, then she'd never have the money to finish her research. Everything, her whole future, her hopes and dreams, her career aspirations, her dissertation research, depended on her staying here in Skyla so that she could finish her work! He didn't understand that. He didn't grasp that a few blisters on her skin wasn't worth losing her whole future over! He most likely wasn't aware that companies usually punished whistleblowers, even in countries where there were laws against such retaliation.

"You will not be fired!" he replied back with a confidence she wished she felt. "In fact, I will guarantee that you are not fired."

She rolled her eyes. "Oh, and you have that kind of power, do you?"

"Yes." It wasn't said with any false bravado and, as Faye looked up at Zantar, she saw that his confidence was backed up by something…perhaps that aura of power was real and not just his arrogance. "Who are you?" she asked, her voice almost a whisper now.

Zantar stared down at Faye, not sure how to answer her. He didn't want her to know who he was. For the first time in his life, he was courting a woman who had no idea who he was. In one way, it was unfortunate that she was an employee of the hotel in which he was staying for the week. But in another way, he was relieved to finally understand why her hands were so badly messed up. The sores and blisters had bothered him the first time he'd seen them but she'd seemed sensitive about them. Now he could use his power to help fix at least that issue.

But instead of explaining how his power was derived, he replied, "I'm just a man who has the power to make a few things right," he told her honestly.

Obviously, that answer wasn't good enough. "What do you do, Zantar?" she asked, and her voice now seemed hesitant.

"Do you trust me?" he asked.

She considered that question for a long moment, then slowly nodded. "Yes," she finally replied.

That one word…it felt like a laser to his lust, inciting it higher than he'd ever thought possible. Lowering his head, he kissed her, trying very hard to be gentle. But the need to kiss her, taste her…hell, to possess her, to somehow imprint himself on her, was an aching need. So perhaps the kiss wasn't as gentle as he'd hoped.

That was brought home when he lifted her into his arms, needing to feel her against his body, absorbing every shiver of excitement running through her. Deepening the kiss, he angled his head, his tongue teasing her lips as he surged inside her mouth, then backing away to nibble at her lower lip, her upper lip before going back for another taste. He wasn't aware of his hands gripping her butt until he heard a sound. Lifting his head, he looked over at a man with a black satchel. He was quickly backing away and Zantar shifted, shielding Faye from the stranger's eyes. He glanced around, but there was a bodyguard right behind the man.

"The doctor has arrived," the guard announced, tilting his head towards the newest man.

Zantar looked down at Faye, wanting to roar with frustration when he saw that her eyes were still cloudy with desire. He wanted to lift her into his arms and carry her off to his bedroom where they could take their time, explore each other a bit more. No, he corrected quickly. He wasn't sure if he could go slowly. At least, not the first time with Faye. But looking down into her confused eyes, he reined himself in. He'd have to go slowly. She obviously wasn't very experienced.

He liked that. He didn't delude himself into thinking she was a virgin, nor did he even care about that. But he liked the idea of waking her sexually, showing her all the ways in which they could pleasure each other.

However, at the moment, he wanted to have this doctor take a look at Faye's hands.

"I am Doctor Sworson," the man announced, extending his hand to shake Zantar's. It was a major breach of protocol and Zantar heard the butler gasp in horror, but Zantar took the doctor's hand, shaking it firmly before turning to Faye. "This is your patient, Doctor. Take a look at her hands and," he looked over the doctor's shoulders to the butler. "Bring me the bottle I left on the counter in your area. Show the doctor what chemicals all of the hotel cleaning staff have been using."

The butler's features drained of color, but he disappeared back to the butler's pantry to retrieve the bottle. Zantar suspected that the bottle had already been swept away into a hiding place by the hotel manager. It wouldn't matter. The evidence of the toxic chemical was all over Faye's hands, and most likely, showing on the hands of the rest of the cleaning crew.

Zantar turned to watch the doctor who was currently tsking over Faye's hands.

"This isn't good," the doctor replied in Arabic.

"Faye doesn't speak the language well enough to understand. Do you speak English?" Zantar asked.

The doctor looked up at Zantar, startled, then looked at Faye.

"I understand a lot," she replied in Arabic, but her words were slow and she mispronounced "*afham*", saying "*aflam*" instead, which meant "films".

Zantar turned to the doctor, silently saying, "Now you understand?"

The doctor smothered his amusement and nodded. In English, he said, "How did you get these blisters, my dear?"

Faye tried curling her fingers to cover up the worst of the sores on the palms of her hands, but the doctor gently opened her hands up, adjusting his wire rimmed glasses as he examined them with his glove-covered hands.

"It's nothing," she replied. "I really should get back to work." Her eyes glanced over towards the door where he suspected the butler was lurking, worried that the man would report everything she said to the general manager.

The doctor shook his head. "Not with these hands," he warned her. "The laws in Skyla clearly state that hospitality workers cannot work with open wounds. And these, my dear, would definitely qualify! This is a health and safety issue."

Faye gasped, her whole body tightening with dread. "No! But…I have to work!"

Zantar shook his head, crossing his arms over his chest. "You will not."

"I must!"

"You can't," he countered.

Faye closed her mouth, pressing her lips together as she fought back an explosion of fury. "You don't understand," she finally gritted out. "I have to work! I need the money!"

The doctor opened up his black bag and pulled out a tube of cream. "This is antibiotic cream," he explained, handing it to her and reaching for his prescription pad. "You need to put this on every one of the sores and scrapes, even the red areas because I suspect that they are about to blister, and this cream will help ease the pressure on the skin cells." Once again, he adjusted his glasses. "Do you have any known allergies to medications?"

Faye shook her head, frustration almost choking her. She was going to ignore the doctor's words and report to work anyway.

The doctor nodded. "I'll inform the hotel that you will be out on sick leave for the next seven days. This cream has a numbing agent as well, so that should ease some of the pain caused by those blisters."

"Seven days?" she whispered, horror causing her words to come out as a mere choked whisper. Thinking about her paycheck coming in just a few days, she wondered how she was going to spread that out to cover the next month's rent, as well as food.

The man must have sensed her panic. "If you are a full-time employee of this hotel," the doctor continued with a gentle expression, "then they are required to cover your lost hourly wages during your sick leave."

Faye shook her head. "I don't qualify. I'm a foreign worker here."

The doctor tilted his head slightly. "Is that what the hotel management told you? That you won't receive any sick leave benefits during your tenure here?"

"Yes," she replied, sick with worry and hunger. She'd had the coffee with Zantar earlier this morning and she had a peanut butter sandwich in her locker. That was all she'd have to eat until she got back to her apartment where she could make a second peanut butter sandwich. In fact, a jar of peanut butter and a skimpy loaf of bread was all she could afford to eat until payday rolled around in a few days!

Damn computer! If her laptop hadn't crashed, this wouldn't be an issue! She'd have plenty of money for food and next month's rent!

"Stop, Faye," Zantar commanded, but his voice was gentle. Almost understanding.

Faye didn't believe for a single moment that he understood what she was going through at this moment. Looking around her at this beautiful, enormous suite, she grasped that the man was disgustingly wealthy. He lived way up here in the clouds! He had no idea what it was like to struggle, to be concerned about where your next meal was coming from! Hell, she hadn't even realized how desperate life could become until this summer when she'd traveled halfway around the world in order to research her dissertation material. Paying the mortgage on her small house back in Georgia, plus her living expenses here…she now more painfully grasped how desperate life could become!

And even in her situation, she had a return plane ticket fully paid for. She could just pack up and leave, go back home and not have to worry about food again.

However, if she did that, Faye would never see Zantar again! That thought was a bit more depressing and scary than not knowing how she would feed herself. Funny how life put worries into perspective.

The tearing of a piece of paper broke through her depressing thoughts and she pulled her eyes away from Zantar to look at the doctor.

"Here you go, my dear," he announced, handing her the prescription.

"I'll take that," Zantar said, taking the paper before Faye could reach for it. "I doubt she'd actually fill the prescription." He didn't bother to glance at Faye when he said that. But Faye grimaced, knowing that he was right. She wouldn't have wasted precious money on medicine for something that wasn't fatal. Another issue that she'd never faced before but people in poverty probably had to deal with every day.

Sometimes, life's lessons sucked!

"I can manage my own medications, Zantar."

His only response was a not-so-subtle lifting of his eyebrows, obviously not believing her.

"Well, if that's all you need," the good doctor said, interrupting their silent argument, "I'll be on my way. I understand that I have many other patients to look at this afternoon." He glanced down at her hands and sighed with a shake of his head. "I don't think I've ever seen hands that bad before. Please take care of your skin. You haven't gotten an infection yet, but those blisters look very bad and very painful. The cream I gave you will help, but protecting your hands for the next week will help more than anything."

And with that, he walked out of the enormous room.

Leaving Faye alone with Zantar.

"I should probably get back to work." Faye glanced up at Zantar, wondering how he would react to that statement. Not well, she realized when she noticed his lips compress with irritation.

"I believe the doctor mentioned that you are now on medical leave," he replied succinctly, crossing his arms over his massive chest and creating the impression of an immovable force.

Faye smiled at the fanciful thought, but her amusement faded quickly when his eyes flared with anger. "I really need to work. And just because the doctor says that the hotel *should* pay me for the hours I'll miss on medical leave, that doesn't mean that it will happen in reality."

"I will ensure that the hotel pays you, and all of the employees, who must miss work because the management staff broke the health and safety laws."

She tilted her head. "How do you know that the hotel broke the law? Isn't it the way of the world that the corporations generally retaliate against the employee?" She did her own arm crossing and glared right back at him. "I'm pretty sure that they will somehow get out of this little debacle. Big corporations always do."

His expression became more determined. "Not always," he muttered.

"Yes," she argued. "They do. The little person, the lowly worker, people like me, rarely get a fair shot in the world. There's corporate corruption everywhere and it's rampant. Anyone who thinks differently is just delusional."

He moved closer, his hands fisting on his hips as he loomed over her now. "I will ensure that you and the others impacted by this toxic mess are compensated fairly. I have connections within the Skyla government," he paused and sighed, rubbing the back of his neck. "Connections that are very high up and they will ensure that everyone who was injured by this chemical cleaning agent is adequately compensated."

"But I'm not a citizen of this country, Zantar. And foreigners, especially workers such as me who have a work visa, have even less ability to fight inequalities. Plus, many of the workers on the cleaning team are women. Females get brushed aside more often than you realize."

He moved even closer, his arm whipping out to wrap around her waist as he pulled her against him. "You will not be brushed aside, Faye," he assured her. "You have my word on that."

She smiled, putting her hand on his arms to steady her balance. "You're a very..." she paused, licking her lips and allowing her eyes to roam over his broad, delectable shoulders "Well, you're hot, Zantar. But I don't think that you're powerful enough to..."

He kissed her, stopping whatever rude comments she might have uttered. He put a hand to the back of her head, keeping her steady. But Faye wasn't pulling away. If anything, she wanted to be closer. She wanted to sink into his strength and feel every part of him against her body. She wanted...him! For the first time in her life, she'd found a man that she wanted to be a part of.

Her fingers lifted higher, touching the skin on his neck then moving to his hair. Soft hair, she absently realized. It was shocking to find something soft on this man that seemed to be hard as granite. Everywhere!

"Your...!" A voice interrupted.

Faye jerked backwards, startled once again and fighting the urge to snap at the next person that interrupted their kiss. It wasn't fair! It was as if the world was conspiring to keep her from kissing this man!

"I'm so sorry!" the man burst out.

Faye looked over her shoulder, needing to glare at the person who had interrupted this time. If it was the doctor again, she would...well, do something really horrible!

"What is it?" Zantar demanded, putting an arm around Faye's waist and pulling her closer.

"Uhh..." This new person looked from Faye to Zantar, obviously wishing that he could simply back out of the room. "The...uh...meeting?" he finished lamely.

Faye felt Zantar's arm tighten around her waist, proving that he was just as irritated as she was at the interruption. But he nodded at the man who backed away. Then Zantar turned to face her again. "I'm sorry, Faye, but I need to go to this meeting. Will you stay here? Will you wait for me to finish?"

She shook her head. "No, I can't do that. I really do need to get back to..." she didn't finish her sentence when his eyes lit up with frustration.

"You're not working Faye," he told her firmly.

"I am." She was just as adamant, needing the hours and the paycheck. "If I don't work, I don't eat." She said that with a flippant tone, not wanting him to know how true that statement really was. She even started moving towards the bedroom where her cart had been left behind. Even though she'd been assigned to clean the penthouse suite, which was significantly easier to clean, she probably had a several other rooms within the suite to finish before her boss came through to inspect.

"You're not working, Faye. In fact, I want you to stay here with me while your hands heal."

Faye paused, startled by his "request". Stay here? In this beautiful suite? Oh goodness, she couldn't imagine living in this kind of luxury, even temporarily!

However, staying here would put her in a very awkward position. "That's not going to happen, Zantar." She was already at the bottom of the staircase when she made that announcement. She turned around and looked at him. "Will you meet me for coffee again tomorrow morning?"

He was just as stubborn. "You will have coffee here. You'll stay the night."

She laughed, shaking her head. "No way. We're not there yet." She glanced around, obviously making sure that they wouldn't be overheard again. "But I hope that we will be there very soon!" And with that, she rushed up the stairs to the bedroom. Looking around, Faye determined that there wasn't anything that truly needed to be cleaned here in the bedroom. The bed had already been made and everything else looked remarkably pristine. She pushed her cart out of the bedroom and back to the employee elevator. She'd check the other rooms in the suite quickly and...!

"You are done for the afternoon, Ms. Lafayette," the butler announced angrily.

Faye looked at him, startled by his words. "But I still have to..."

The hotel manager stepped into the small space from the elevator that had just opened up, his eyes glaring at her. "You need to leave the hotel immediately!"

Faye stared at the man, a choking sensation filling her. She was being fired! She'd caused problems and now she was fired!

"I understand," she said with a defiant lift of her head. She'd done nothing wrong! But there were always consequences for the worker-bees in this world. It didn't matter if those consequences were unfair. "I'll just get my personal belongings out of my locker."

Oh, she was going to give Zantar an earful tomorrow when she met him for coffee! Not that she could afford coffee! Not anymore!

Chapter 6

Zantar walked into the conference room, irritated and ready to punch someone. He didn't want to be here. He wanted to be back at his hotel with Faye. He just knew that she was going to leave his suite. And if she left the suite, she'd probably keep on working. *Ealayk allaena!* He resisted the urge to turn around and head back to the hotel. He wanted to demand that she put more medicine on her hands, maybe even bandage them up so that...no, the wounds had all closed up, but they still looked painful.

Why the hell hadn't he asked about her hands before? Right. He had asked about her hands and she'd...what had Faye said? What had been her excuse at the time? He couldn't remember. Although, he remembered being entranced by her smile and her eyes. Those blue eyes were startling and intense. He could see all of her emotions in those eyes. He wanted to lose himself in her eyes. And her body. And her smile! He wanted to see that smile sitting across from him every morning and every evening. He wanted to pull her into his arms and make love to her, show her that there was more to life than just research and work!

Sighing, he shook his head as he wondered about these intense feelings. He'd known her for only a few days now. How could he feel so much for a woman he barely knew?

Zantar accepted that he didn't have to know everything about Faye to know *her*. He could feel her, sense her. He wanted to be with her. What the hell was it about Faye that called to him? The other women who had passed through his life had been there for one purpose! He'd never allowed any woman to interfere with his focus.

He almost laughed at that last thought. He wasn't "allowing" Faye to do anything. Hell, he'd love it if he could stop "allowing" her to interfere! Then he could concentrate and get some work done. If he could concentrate more fully on the issue that had brought him to Skyla, then perhaps he could get back home!

And leave Faye here?

No. No way in hell! He'd just have to figure out how to keep her with him. He wanted her in his life. Sighing, he accepted that he had... feelings...for Faye. What those feelings were, he wasn't sure. And not something he cared to delve into too deeply.

"Sheik al Abouss!" a male voice called out.

Zantar turned, watching as Sheik Astir and Sheik Goran stepped into the room. "We're just waiting on Nasir to arrive."

Sheik Nasir bin Zaminista was ruler of Minar which was located to the west of Sklya. Why was he coming to this meeting as well? That's very odd, Zantar thought, more confused than ever.

Another thought occurred to him as he watched Astir speak to his personal assistant. Did the man realize that there was something going on between Ayla, Astir's youngest sister, and Nasir? Zantar had seen the interest in the couple the last time all four leaders had gotten together for a conference. Ayla had come along and...yes, there had definitely been tension between the lovely woman and Nasir.

Astir finished his private conversation and turned to Zantar and Goran. "I apologize for that," he explained and stepped deeper into the conference room.

"Has something changed since earlier this week?" Zantar asked. He crossed his arms over his chest, not interested in the romantic issues of his friends. Goran was marrying Astir's middle sister and Nasir was interested in the younger sister. But that had nothing to do with him. In his mind, he didn't need to be here in Skyla any longer, except to spend more time with Faye. This meeting had taken him away from her and he was irritated that he wasn't still with her.

Ignoring their idle conversations as they waited for Nasir, he pushed the agenda by saying, "I thought that we determined a few days ago that the issues were resolved. Why did you ask to speak with me again?"

Goran smiled and Zantar wanted to slug the man for being so cheerful. Glancing over at Astir, he wondered if the other man would stop him. Probably, he thought with grim resignation. Astir's gaze seemed concerned about something, and Zantar suspected that his concerns had nothing to do with Goran dating the man's sister.

Astir paused to glare at the other man, but he pushed away from the wall and walked over to a hidden panel. "We have new information that might concern Citran." He touched a button and the wall behind Zantar slid open to reveal a large map of their three countries with Silar at the top, Skyla off to the east, Citran to the south, and Minar, a fourth country, to the west. A moment later, the ruler of Minar stepped into the room, firmly closing the door behind him.

"I apologize for my tardiness," Sheik Nasir bin Zaminista asked, walking over to the screen. "What have I missed?"

"Nothing," Astir replied, giving that man a strange glance that Zantar couldn't interpret. "We were just bringing Zantar up to speed on the situation."

"Situation?" Zantar asked, his eyebrows lifting higher while his muscles tightened as he dismissed the strange tension between the other three men. He glanced over at the map. "What the hell is going on?" he demanded, thinking about the briefing he'd just had with his intelligence chief. Something was happening near the border towns along the south side of his country. If his chief hadn't mentioned that something strange was going on, he wouldn't even be here. He'd actually thought that it was perhaps Goran's military causing trouble in that area.

"It's not me," Goran assured him with a calm voice, seeming to read Zantar's mind. "Something is going on down here," he explained, stepping forward to point at the electronic visual of the region. "It's affecting all four of our countries."

Nasir stepped closer to the map, pointing to the region. "I've received word recently about disturbances here," he announced, pointing to several small villages along the border between Minar and Citran." He ran his finger along the border.

"What kind of disturbances?" Zantar demanded. His attention was caught, and he leaned forward, his eyes taking in additional details now that he had a new clue.

Nasir turned to look at the other man, shaking his head slightly. "We don't really understand. The information we're getting from people who live in the area say that there are occasional seismic events they can feel, but nothing like a real earthquake."

Zantar's eyes narrowed. "How would they know what an earthquake feels like?"

Astir nodded. "That was our concern. And no one said that the disturbances were actually earthquakes. But ever since the incident in Silar where a town collapsed, we're taking these seismic-seeming issues seriously." He shook his head, rubbing the back of his neck. "Unfortunately, we don't know what they are now. Originally, Goran and I thought the illegal mining was affecting only Skyla and Silar. You both heard about the town that collapsed into what we thought was a sinkhole several months back," he explained, his eyes serious now as all three men listened intently. "It turned out to be an illegal mining operation that was drilling and extracting efiasia, a mineral that can be used to build cheap microchips for computers. But the mineral was too close to the surface and the mining company's operations caused the whole town to collapse into the Earth." He looked at each man separately, letting that information sink in.

Sheik Goran nodded, pulling everyone's attention to him. "And then I was kidnapped in order to focus everyone's attention on my absence and," Goran looked over to his future brother-in-law, both men's expressions grim and determined, "Princess Calista's."

Zantar's eyes sharpened. "My information was that both of you were taking some time away from your public duties in order to get to know each other a bit better." He pulled back, his arms crossing over his chest. "Now you're telling us that you and your future bride were kidnapped?"

"Exactly," Goran confirmed with a firm nod. "Whoever is behind these mining problems keeps coming up with new company names for their illegal mining efforts, but," he tilted his head towards Astir, "we think that the activities are all caused by one company."

"But you don't know who?" Nasir asked.

Astir and Goran both shook their heads. "Not yet," Astir replied.

Zantar sighed. "Okay, so you think that there are some additional, illegal efforts that could affect Citran?" he asked. He turned to look at Nasir. "And why are you here? What's Minar's connection to these debacles?"

Astir and Goran leaned into the map a bit more. Astir explained, "My mining agency investigators have determined that the efiasia deposits are enormous." He looked at each man for a moment, then pointed to the map. "The deposit covers all four of our countries. Whoever is behind these efforts, they aren't stopping."

Zantar thought about the unexplained seismic activity as well as the trucks that had been seen traveling in strange areas. Areas where there shouldn't be large trucks. "And you think that, whoever is doing this, has decided to reach the deposit through Citran now." It wasn't a question.

Goran nodded. "That's our assumption." He turned to Nasir. "We also suspect that, if this company fails in Citran, you might be next."

Nasir sighed, rubbing his jawline. "So far, I haven't heard anything about illegal mining operations in Minar."

Zantar shook his head. "It doesn't have to be mining," he announced. He pointed to the town he'd just been briefed on. "There are several dozen large trucks here," he said, pointing to a small dot on the map.

"My investigators haven't seen any drilling equipment. Not yet."

Astir smiled slightly. "But you have some suspicions?"

Zantar nodded, finally understanding what prompted his invitation to this additional meeting. "I didn't believe the news about you and Princess Calista going off to have some private time." He looked over at Astir with a chuckle. "I know you," he said to his friend. "You'd never let your sister go off, alone, with this brute."

Astir chuckled, but didn't deny the comment. Goran didn't react in any way, he simply glared right back at Zantar.

Nasir stepped in. "But after news about Silar and Skyla's problems, you'll start digging into the truck issue a bit more?"

Zantar shrugged slightly. "I think it would be prudent. I can't stop a company from driving trucks along the highway, though. However, my agents can be a bit more aggressive and find out what they're up to."

Goran pointed to the long road. "My investigators are interested in the trucks as well. At first, we'd thought maybe someone was stealing oil."

Zantar tilted his head slightly as they all studied the map. "That wouldn't make sense. There are easier and more efficient ways to steal from oil rigs rather than tunneling underground. Reaching the oil pipelines is easier than most people realize."

Astir nodded in agreement. "Exactly. We discarded that idea pretty quickly." He pointed to the area on the map where their four countries touched. "Besides, the areas where the disturbances have been reported aren't near any drilling operations or pipelines. It would require hundreds of miles of underground tunnels and piping in order to siphon off the oil. It just doesn't make any sense."

"So what have you come up with?" Zantar asked, intrigued and more than a little eager to find who was doing this and stopping them. So far, it hadn't affected his country very much. At least, he didn't think so. There were reports of something going on, but...! "My intelligence chief mentioned a series of trucks moving from here late at night," he said, pointing on a site right on the edge of the border, "that are driving eastward towards this area." He let his finger move over the satellite image towards the mountains. "But we haven't figured out where the trucks came from or where they are going."

Astir moved, looking at the map. "Trucks going from the middle of nowhere to the mountains? Why the hell would they do that? There's nothing out there."

"Nothing that we know of," Astir filled in, his voice cautious.

They all turned and looked towards the man, but no one had any immediate answers. Everyone's eyes narrowed as they each considered the possibilities.

Finally Astir spoke up. "I think it's time that we all get our intelligence people together. We're working separately. But if we pool our resources, maybe we could figure this out more effectively."

Goran smiled slightly, nodding his head with agreement. "I know that's a good idea and would probably be the most efficient. But I don't think that our intelligence heads would play well together." The four of them laughed at the idea of the super-secretive heads of each of their intelligence agencies actually sharing information with each other. It just wouldn't happen.

"That's why I brought the four of us together. Astir and I met together initially when we first discovered something was going on." Astir explained.

Goran chuckled. "That's when I ran into his lovely sister again, which is why Astir is an angry bear." The other two men glanced over at Astir and he merely lifted an eyebrow. Nasir and Zantar both nodded with understanding. "Which is why I think we should each speak with our various groups, then come back together so that the four of us can share our information."

"That would be smoother," Nasir replied. He looked towards Zantar.

Goran continued, "Astir and I have already started sharing information with each other and are on friendly terms, despite Astir's continued growling." There was a heavy sigh and Zantar glanced over at Astir, smothering his amusement when the big man rolled his eyes. Zantar noticed that Astir didn't deny the statement. Which, in this kind of a situation, was as good as confirmation.

He then turned his attention towards Nasir. "Do you think that the four of us might work together to stop another tragedy?"

Zantar and Nasir both glanced at each other, both of them standing with their feet braced wide and their arms crossed over their chests. Zantar pinned the other man with a look for a long moment. They'd never been friends, but they hadn't been enemies either. There had always been a healthy competition between the four countries, although there hadn't been any violence. At least, not for several centuries.

Nasir was eyeing Zantar in the same way, both men taking each other's measure. In the end, both men nodded sharply, agreeing to cooperate.

"Excellent," Astir replied, clapping his hands together. "Let's get started."

For the next several hours, the four men brainstormed, excused themselves to private rooms where they could speak with their intelligence chiefs, then came back to the table with new information. Each time one of the leaders left, they arrived back at the table with another piece of the puzzle. It wasn't that anyone was holding back on information. It was merely that each new piece of information resulted in more clues, bringing a bit more clarity to the larger picture.

Food was brought in but barely consumed. Pots of coffee transitioned to beer and wine. Around midnight, they all stared at the map. The conference room table had been shoved out of the way to make room to walk and examine the satellite image on the wall. The chairs had been pushed around the room, papers scattered wildly over the polished surface of the table, but the four men kept coming back to the large, digital map on the wall, each of them discussing the possibilities.

Around one in the morning, Zantar was speaking with the head of his intelligence office and stopped. "An explosion?" he asked. The word caused everyone in the room to stop speaking. They all looked over at him and Zantar shook his head. "What about an underground explosion?" he asked, speaking into the phone as well as to the three men in the room.

The other leaders stared at him for a long moment, the silence almost shattering as they processed the possibilities. Moments later, they all started speaking into their phones once again. Astir wrote something down on a sticky note, then smacked it onto the map. "Underground explosion!" He also wrote "Didn't register on Richter scale" on the bottom.

At the same time, Nasir was on the phone with his Mineral Resource expert who was explaining that "Mining explosions rarely create a measurement on the Richter scale unless the explosion is right over the measuring equipment. "The only exception to that rule was if the explosion was created by an underground nuclear explosion. Those would register on the scale, and would most likely even produce aftershocks."

The men all stopped at that point, each of them ending their calls and coming together. Four men, standing in front of the digital image, hands fisted on their hips as they stared at the information they'd gathered so far. There were sticky notes all over the map. Some of the information on the notes was pertinent. Other notes contained something someone discovered and put it up for consideration – but now that they knew...or suspected...what was going on, those notes were most likely irrelevant.

Nasir snatched several notes away, tossing them into the nearby trashcan. The trash would later be incinerated for security reasons.

"So narrowing down the possibilities, we have someone tunneling under our four countries and..." He paused, then picked up the digital pen that would draw lines over the satellite image. "Look at this!" He used the pen to electronically draw a circle around the areas where unexplained issues had been detected. Those issues included a large region where the businesses had suddenly reported closing, a disproportionate and sudden spike in housing sales, many of which hadn't been sold so the prices had been reduced, and local law enforcement authorities had reported a larger than average spike in violent crimes, especially in areas that had previously been considered extremely low crime sections.

"We've been looking at these issues separately," Nasir explained, his eyes focusing on his lines as well as the small villages and towns that were within the triangle he'd drawn. "What if we look at them from a bird's eye view?" He picked up a piece of paper, then looked at the image again, drawing a few more lines.

When they all stepped back, they looked at the connecting areas where there had been unexplained sales or crime spikes, there was a very visible circle as well as a road that led into and out of the perimeter. The same unexplained issues were happening along the road heading into the mountains, and even some of the small mountain towns had been hit with some odd incidents. The lines made the connections more obvious.

"I'll be damned," Zantar whispered.

"Who would do this?" Astir growled.

"And why?" Goran snapped.

Nasir sighed, stepping in front of the image and facing the men. "I don't know. But now that we know the what, let's focus on the why." He put the electronic pen down. "Let's continue this investigation tomorrow."

The men all nodded, agreeing with taking a break. They'd been going for hours now, and it was time for everyone to take a step back and process what they'd learned today.

"Tomorrow, we'll start fresh." Astir lifted his cup of coffee in the air as a salute, then looked down at the cold brew and grimaced with distaste. "I'll ensure that we have hot coffee tomorrow as well.'

The other men laughed, shaking their heads. Normally, a servant would come into meetings to ensure that coffee and food options were available, hot, and edible. But because of the sensitive nature of this investigation, all four men had agreed to keep everyone out, including their personal bodyguards, in order to ensure absolute privacy.

One by one, they walked out of the conference room, each silent now as they went in different directions. Zantar was wondering if Faye had remained at the hotel as he'd hoped. But he doubted it. He'd asked, but she was such an independent woman. She'd probably considered his request as a dare to go back to wherever she currently lived and figure out how to survive on her own without a job.

Stubborn woman, he thought as he anticipated meeting her for coffee tomorrow morning. He glanced down at his watch, cringing when he realized that he'd only get about three hours of sleep before meeting the lovely woman.

Ealayk allaena, as soon as he saw Faye, Zantar vowed to figure out how to get her to move into his hotel suite. Maybe he could offer her some sort of job. She was a smart, creative woman. He was positive that there would be a position for her within his government.

As soon as that thought hit him, he wondered why he hadn't thought of it before this moment. Probably because her presence caused him to think of…other things. If he'd been thinking properly, he might have come up with the idea the first day he'd met her. Or more accurately, the first day he'd seen the damage to her hands. *Aljahim*, he should have asked about that damage on the first day. But he'd been too overwhelmed with her eyes. And her lips. Well, all of her, actually.

The cell phone's ringing woke Scott up. He looked around, trying to figure out what time it was while answering the phone with a growled, "What the hell do you want?"

Rubbing his eyes, he picked up the watch sitting on the bedside table, squinting as he tried to read the numbers. Damn watch! He'd paid over fifty thousand dollars for the damn thing, and he still couldn't read the stupid numbers! All he knew was that it was some time around two o'clock in the morning. Or maybe it was ten minutes after some other hour. It was still dark out. That's all that mattered, he thought, mentally going through a litany of expletives.

"You told me that you had the situation under control," a creaky, angry voice snapped through the phone.

It was the cold, almost friendly tone of voice that got through to him and caused him to jerk awake, jackknifing up in bed.

Soft, feminine hands smoothed over his back but he jerked away from the touch, shoving the irritating hands away. He felt his elbow hit something and he heard a soft gasp but couldn't take the time to figure out what he'd done.

"Sir!" Scott croaked out, trying to control the panic that was now creating a tight band around his chest, making it hard to breathe. There wasn't much that scared him in this world. But this man…Harvey Neville was one of the most terrifying, most inhumane people Scott had ever encountered. He was also the wealthiest. Of all the people who topped the wealthiest charts, Scott suspected that this man was worth ten times more than all of them. No one knew about this guy's work though. He was evil even beyond anything Scott could ever imagine.

The freak paid well though. That was the only reason Scott had signed up to work for the bastard!

"People are interfering with my business, Mr. Roland. I don't like people interfering. You told me that you could handle the situation in Citran and the surrounding countries more effectively than your two predecessors. Now I'm discovering that you lied!"

Scott swallowed, not sure what the hell was going on. "I assure you, Mr. Neville, that everything is under control. I'm here in the capital monitoring the news from my sources inside the government. The trucks in Citran are able to come and go from the underground staging area easily. They leave during the night hours when everyone is asleep. The efiasia is being excavated at high quantities and shipped out in your containers. We're actually ahead of our delivery schedule at the moment."

There was a hissing sound and Scott suspected that the man was inhaling through his narrow nasal passages. "And the towns? The residents will be out of the way on schedule so the real work can be accomplished? That first idiot, Jeffrey something-or-other, thought he had the town under control and look how that turned out!" The man paused for a scary moment. "I don't want anything to hinder my progress. That mineral is essential to my plans, Mr. Roland. You might be ahead of schedule now, but anything could change that status."

"Yes!" Scott assured him, mentally going through his list of potential obstacles. He stood up and grabbed the woman's clothes, pulling open the hotel room door and throwing her clothes out. She squeaked in fury, but Scott ignored her, taking her arm and pushing her out as well, all the while assuring Mr. Neville that everything was going as planned.

"You bastard!" the prostitute hissed, grabbing the skimpy dress she'd worn on the street corner the previous evening, pressing it against her naked breasts. Scott ignored her, turning and tripping over something. When he looked down at the floor, he saw that the woman's ridiculous platform shoes were lying there. He might have tossed them there last night after he'd had sex with the woman. He vaguely remembered telling her to keep them on.

"Yes, sir, the trucks are carrying dirt at a rate of five thousand tons a day. The underground explosions are effective at breaking up the rocks to expose the efiasia veins, but since everything is being done underground, there isn't any evidence that anything is changing up on ground level. Even if the satellites took images of the area, they wouldn't notice any changes. The trucks are coming and going through underground passageways that hide their movements." He yanked open the hotel room door once again and threw the shoes out, slamming the door closed again. He heard the woman screech again and suspected that one of the shoes had hit her. But he didn't have the time, nor the inclination, to sooth her hurt feelings. He was too busy not getting killed in some horrific way by this man's minions.

"That all sounds perfect, Mr. Roland." There was a long pause and Scott wondered if the man had hung up on him. But then Scott heard papers shifting in the background and clenched the phone more tightly. "It has come to my attention that the leader of..." another pause, "Citran...is visiting the capital of Skyla. I think he should be the first leader to sign the mining documents. Most of the minerals I want are underneath his country and since he's away from Citran, he might not know what's going on. It should be easy enough to get him to sign the contracts so that I am covered in the case of any...issues." Another pause and Scott wondered if the man was certifiably insane. "Get Sheik al Abouss to sign the papers or get him out of the way." Then there was a muted click, and the line went dead.

Scott glanced at the phone, ensuring that the call had truly been terminated before letting out a long breath as he fell backwards on to the bed. For a moment, he stared up at the ceiling, wondering if he should just cut his losses and get out of town, find another job. One that wouldn't end with his excruciating death.

Unfortunately, he'd spent almost all of what he'd earned, so leaving right now, with just the cash left over from his last payment, would mean he wasn't quite as well off as he'd like to be. Scott knew that he had an issue with spending. He liked shiny things and liked living like a king. He loved the way people treated him when he paid for their drinks or meals, or when he found a pleasing prostitute to soothe his sore muscles. He chuckled at that last thought.

Should he just get away? He considered the option, but then he remembered of all the lovely money still to be earned and smiled, opening his eyes. Yeah, Scott knew that he was a greedy bastard. But he didn't care. He liked money. Correction, he liked all of the things he could buy with his money.

Vaguely, he wondered if the woman was still out in the hallway. He remembered her tongue from last night. How had that woman learned to do those things? She was an artist. Just thinking about the things she'd done to him made his body react. He wanted another round. Hell, he wanted a few more rounds. That was why he'd told the woman she could stay last night. Unfortunately, he'd fallen asleep after that first round and...! He sat up again, looking around for his pants. Finding them laying on the ground, he quickly rifled through the pockets, then muttered a string of curses. "That bitch!" he growled when he discovered that the large amount of cash he'd kept in his wallet was gone.

He shook his head, gritting his teeth as he wondered where the hell the woman had hidden his money! She'd been naked when he'd kicked her out a few minutes ago. And that dress…surely there hadn't been any pockets on that dress where she could have hidden the money.

Walking over to the doorway, he yanked open the door for the third time in less than five minutes. Yeah, it was two o'clock in the morning. So what if the people had been sleeping right across the hallway from him. He'd been robbed! They could damn well wake up and bitch about the noise, for all he cared!

When Scott realized that the woman wasn't around any longer, he muttered more expletives as he slammed the door closed. "What the hell am I supposed to do for money now?" he growled. He'd spent every penny he'd earned so far, which was quite an accomplishment since he'd earned an enormous amount from this job. But he had needs! The watch, the prostitute, new clothes, not to mention this hotel room. Scott could have saved a bit of money by leasing a rental, but he didn't like to be tied down. He needed to be able to just head out on a whim when he needed to leave. It was easier to get out of town when one only needed to grab a backpack. Plus, he went back and forth from the capital in Skyla to the work site in Citran, ensuring that everyone was doing their job properly. Hotels were more convenient all around.

Thinking of convenience, it was better if all of his body parts remained on his body. He didn't doubt that Neville would hunt him down and do horrifying things to him if he left.

So he had to ensure that his plan would continue to work. Mentally, Scott sorted through his plans to get rid of the town's residents, or anyone, that might either report the odd number of trucks on the roads to the government, or turn in the mining company's operations because of noise or pollution, or in a worst-case scenario, get sick because of the toxic chemicals the mining company was using to filter out the minerals they needed from the rocks and dirt. It was similar to the way gold mining companies now used cyanide to leech the gold from the earth, and it wasn't a happy result for the environment.

The efiasia his teams were digging up would eventually be used to make the microchips for computers. Yeah, there were better, more effective minerals the computer companies could use, but Harvey Neville was a cheap bastard, more than ready to make a knock-off, poorly constructed product if he thought it would expand the profit margins. Plus, as long as the data transferred properly through the whatchamacallits in the belly of the computer, the people who bought the computers didn't want to know how it worked.

Lower costs meant higher profits. As far as Scott was concerned, it was a win-win for everyone. Consumers got cheaper and faster computers, and he got more money. Who cares if a few thousand people were forced from their homes during the process? This was progress, and operations like his had happened throughout the history of the world. The only people who were remembered during the evolutions of business were the people who made the money.

Scott was determined to be one of those people who makes a ton of money. And he didn't care who he had to step on to get there!

Chapter 7

Faye waited, wringing her hands as she looked up and down the street for Zantar. He'd wanted her to stay in his hotel suite yesterday, but she hadn't. She'd gone off and...well, the hotel manager had been livid with her! He'd told her to get the hell out of the hotel.

She was going to have to go home to Georgia, she thought. Faye had no idea how she was going to finish her dissertation, but maybe there was some way. Perhaps she could...maybe she could...? Closing her eyes in defeat, she inhaled slowly and carefully, trying to avoid another round of angry tears. She had no options. Leaving Skyla at this point in her research would be devastating. But she'd figure something out. She had to!

And yet, at the moment, her biggest concern was never seeing Zantar again. The hour or so with him in the morning had quickly become the highlight of her day. He was excitement and danger, all rolled up into a humongous male package.

What if he didn't show up? What if he left the country without any word? What if she'd angered him so much that he'd simply left Skyla? Her heart thudded in her chest at the possibility.

No! No, he hadn't left! She could feel it. He was still here. Somewhere! He had to be!

Faye paced in front of the coffee shop for another ten minutes, glancing at her phone to look at the time about every thirty seconds. When he hadn't arrived by their normal time...Faye's heart sank. Bowing her head, she accepted that she'd pushed him too far. And yet, she couldn't have stayed at the hotel suite. Not only would the management have kicked her out, but she simply wouldn't allow herself to be dependent on a man! Doing so would have violated everything she believed in. She had to be strong. She had to make her own way in this world!

Efin walked over to her, and Faye just about jumped a foot in the air when he tapped her on her shoulder. Gasping, she put a hand to her heart as she tried to calm her racing nerves. "Sorry!" she sighed, looking at the cute waiter.

"You wish for coffee?" he asked in his normal broken English.

Faye turned and looked down the street. "No," she replied when she didn't see a big, black SUV approaching. "No, I think I'll skip the…" Before she could finish the statement, the black SUV turned the corner and Faye's heart leapt in excitement! "He's here!" she whispered.

Efin turned startled eyes towards the black SUV and he straightened his shoulders. "I get coffee!" he whispered, backing up and moving hurriedly towards the interior of the café.

Faye didn't pay him any attention. Her heart and her eyes were too focused on Zantar as he stepped out of the back of the SUV. He walked over to her, buttoning his suit jacket as he approached. "You didn't stay last night," he grumbled, looking down at her with a strange look in his dark eyes.

"I didn't," she replied, stating the obvious. "I couldn't."

"Why couldn't you?" he asked gently, moving closer. They were barely an inch apart and she could smell all of him. Her body reacted to his presence, coming alive in ways she'd never thought possible.

"Because…" she stopped, her eyes staring into his dark gaze. "You're here," she whispered, her lips slowly curling into a smile. "I thought that you wouldn't want to have coffee with me anymore."

"I want you," he replied, and Faye wondered if he meant wanting to have coffee with her or wanting…her! She swallowed.

"I'm glad," she whispered, wishing that she wasn't revealing so much by her breathy tone. She needed to be strong. Assertive. She needed to appear confident and defiant! And yet, all she wanted was for him to pull her into his arms and kiss her just like he'd done last night.

"I can't kiss you," he stated.

Faye was so startled and so hurt, she blinked, pulling back slightly. She didn't realize that her smile disappeared suddenly but she lowered her lashes, trying to hide the hurt his statement created inside of her. "I understand," she lied.

"No, you don't," he said, putting a hand under her elbow as he led her over to their table. "But you will. Soon." He pulled out a chair for her and Faye sat down, wishing that she understood this man. "Very soon, you will understand a great deal, Faye."

Zantar moved to the other side of the table, wishing that he could take her into his arms and kiss her until she was completely unaware of the world. He couldn't stop thinking about how she'd reacted to his kiss yesterday, looking flushed and flustered. Beautiful! However, yesterday, they'd been in his suite. They'd been protected by the privacy of the penthouse. He couldn't kiss her here in the street for fear of someone taking a picture of their embrace. Anything that salacious would be all over the tabloids by the time he finished his first cup of coffee. And he couldn't do that to Faye. She was too sweet and too unaware of who he was, too ignorant of the impact a relationship with him might have on her future.

"I will kiss you after our dinner tonight," he told her. "And then I will drive you home and you will show me where you live."

Faye was startled by this pronouncement, her eyes widening as she said, "I will?"

He chuckled at her sarcastic tone. "Yes. I checked in with the hotel. They assured me that you will be paid for the hours you will miss over the next week. And when your medical leave is over, you will be welcomed back to work. There will be no blemish on your work history."

Faye's eyes widened with that news, and he felt a surge of satisfaction. "Oh!" He watched her eyes, amazed at how they turned an even deeper blue with that assurance. "Thank you."

"You shouldn't have to thank me, Faye. The hotel management was in the wrong for using chemicals that were too harsh for the way they were being used. I've also informed the correct agency here in Skyla to look into your hotel, as well as the other hotels, to ensure that the management teams are protecting the employees with proper care and supervision."

She blinked, stared down at her coffee cup for a long moment, then asked, "You have that much power?"

He tilted his head ever so slightly. "Yes, Faye. I have powerful connections. I understand that you don't fully grasp my reach. But soon, you will understand."

She laughed, shaking her head. "I doubt it," she replied. "I don't think I could ever understand that kind of power. I'm just..." She stopped and sighed, folding her hands on her lap before she lifted her eyes up to him again. "I'm a school teacher, Zantar. Even if I earn my PhD, then I'll still be a school teacher, although, hopefully, I'll be teaching students who are more interested in art than the easy grade most of my current students hope for when taking my class." Her shoulders slumped slightly. "I doubt I could understand what it's like to issue an edict and have that edict followed through on." She grinned slightly. "I can barely get my students to do their homework."

Efin arrived with a tray of pastries and steaming coffee, then quickly backed away.

Zantar didn't like the defeated look on her lovely, normally vibrant features. "Soon, Faye. Very soon, you will understand a great deal."

She blinked, looking over at him. "Why?"

He shook his head. "Don't worry about that. Let me see your hands. Did you get the prescription filled? Do your hands feel better today?"

Faye laughed, rolling her eyes at his dictatorial commands, but she lifted her hands from under the table and showed him. "They are much improved. And they don't hurt nearly as much as they did yesterday," she told him. "The cream that the doctor gave me really did the job."

"I'm relieved." He took her hands in his, marveling at how small and slender her hands were. They were pretty, despite the sores and blisters and redness everywhere. "You have lovely hands, Faye," he told her.

"I don't," she replied, her fingers curling up in an effort to hide the horror that her skin had become. "I used to have pretty hands. Strong hands. I could draw just about anything," she told him. "I wasn't an inspired artist. I wasn't someone who could generate shock waves in the world with my paintings, but I can draw a picture that is passably good." She shook her head as she turned her hands over, staring at the rough areas where the blisters were healing. "The chemicals at the hotel really did some damage." She looked up at him. "Thank you for your intervention. Even if the hotel management doesn't pay me for the hours I'll miss over the next week, I will still be grateful to you. There are so many other employees who work there that deserve better working conditions. The poor really don't have a great deal of power. They get trampled on often enough and, slowly, they lose their will to fight for what's right."

"You stood up for them, Faye."

She laughed, shaking her head. "No way, Zantar. You did. I was the one begging you to leave it alone. You have a very selective memory if you are saying I did anything other than cower and beg you to leave it alone. I was too worried about losing my job and my meager income." She sighed, pushing her hands back under the table where he couldn't see them any longer. "And I'm truly grateful for your help with the medical leave as well as being able to keep my job. Without that income, I couldn't finish my dissertation research. So thank you!"

"It is my honor," he replied. "Tell me more about your research. Will you spend more time at the museum over the next week now that you don't have to work at the hotel?"

Relief that she didn't have to leave Skyla, that she could continue her research hit her with a thud. Her smile brightened and she almost laughed. "Yes!" Efin arrived with their coffee, smiling and bowing as he backed away.

Immediately, she sat up and poured for both of them, adding cream and sugar to her cup, but leaving his without any additions.

"What will you do with the extra time over the next week?"

Faye wrapped her hands around the now-warm ceramic cup of coffee. "I can't wait to get into the details a bit more. I always had to pay attention to the time so I could hurry out of the museum in time to get to the hotel for my shift. But now I can just lose myself in the paintings and maybe find more answers. I intend to spend half of my time at the museum and half of it in the library."

"And your evenings with me," he finished for her, lifting his cup of coffee to take a long, satisfied sip.

Her smile widened and she tilted her head slightly. "And my evenings with you," she agreed softly.

They talked about her research after that. Faye explained about the newest symbols she'd found in the paintings. She discovered that he'd looked up information on her artist and knew about the paintings she'd referenced during their conversation. It warmed her heart that he'd taken the time to do that. It proved to her that she was special to him and not just some woman he didn't give a fig about.

Her phone alarm went off and she stopped it, then looked up at him, resigned. "I'd better get going. The museum director will be wondering where I am."

"I will drive you to this museum," he stated.

Faye laughed, shaking her head. "No way," she pulled back. "We go in the opposite direction. It would be out of your way to drive me there."

He leaned forward, taking her hand as he walked her towards the waiting SUV. "I will drive you to the museum and I will examine these paintings with you." He lifted a hand when she started to speak. "I won't interrupt your work, Faye," he told her gently, but firmly. "I just want to see these paintings. I looked them up online, but I prefer seeing things in person."

She smiled at that. "I guess that would be okay. I forgot to ask the director about letting you see them yesterday. However, I can't imagine that Mr. Latro would mind if someone else came in to see the paintings. He's very excited about others learning of this artist's brilliance."

He held her hand as the backdoor of the SUV was opened for them. "This will also allow me to kiss you."

Faye tripped with his words, but Zantar merely held her closer, enjoying the feeling of her soft curves against his body. Her breasts brushed against him, and he wanted to pull her into his arms right here and then kiss her and feel that passion explode around them just as it had yesterday. Thankfully, he was able to restrain himself long enough to help her into the SUV. But the moment that the doors were closed, he pulled her into his arms and kissed her, unmindful of the driver and guard who were sitting in the front seat. He didn't care. Zantar knew that if he didn't kiss Faye now, right this moment, he would burst into flames of frustration!

She slipped into his arms as if she'd been hoping for the same thing. Her slender arms twined around his neck and she lifted her face to his kiss. He didn't hesitate now. Kissing her was more important than breathing!

As their lips touched, he felt the heat explode around them. She was on fire, as was he. They shifted, he held her hips against his, her body moving against him as her mouth open to him, his tongue sliding inside her mouth to explore and taste.

She made sexy little sounds in the back of her throat, moving closer, as if their kiss wasn't enough. It wasn't enough for him either, and those sounds were making him crazy! He wanted to tear off her clothes and discover the womanly curves underneath. He wanted to taste her, smell her, watch as she exploded around him. He wanted to imprint himself on her so that she couldn't breathe without him close by. Because that's how he felt. Every moment yesterday had been an irritating mess, not just because of the investigation into someone's criminal efforts, but because Faye wasn't by his side. Because she hadn't been at the hotel, waiting for him. Because he hadn't been able to hold her and tell her about all of the things he'd discovered, nor had he been able to hear what she'd learned about her artist.

Everything about this woman intrigued him, including the way her fingers curled around his neck, pulling him closer, her lips teasing his, her pretty, white teeth biting his lower lip, her soft sighs or shocked gasps when he touched a new place on her body.

Too soon, his driver pulled up outside of the museum. Zantar wanted to fire the man for being so damn efficient! *Alleanat ealaa alrajul!* Couldn't he have taken the long route there?

Slowly, he pulled away, but paused to nibble along her neck and her ear, eliciting a few more gasps of pleasure before he stopped.

Not nearly satisfied, Zantar enjoyed the sweet sigh of frustration when she realized that he wasn't about to kiss her again. Her eyes were still closed, her soft lips parted, as if waiting for another kiss. He was just about to kiss her, to give into the urge, when she opened her eyes to try and figure out why he'd stopped.

Those blue eyes weren't very focused as she turned her head, looking out through the tinted windows. Suddenly, she stiffened on his lap and if his hands weren't holding her hips, Faye might have tumbled to the floor of the SUV. "We're here!" she exclaimed and Zantar's frustration cooled slightly. It was hard to be angry when she appeared to be just as affected as he was.

"Oh my gosh!" she gasped, shifting on the leather seat in an ungraceful move. Zantar clenched his teeth as another bolt of lust surged through him with that movement. He gripped the edge of the seat for a long moment, irritated when she simply picked up her cotton bag and slid towards the doorway. She jerked the handle, pushing it open and stepping out into the morning sunshine. But Zantar moved a bit more slowly, needing to get his body back under control before he stepped out into the public. His guards would know what was going on even though the partition between himself and them had been closed.

Through sheer force of will, he pulled his mind out of the lust induced stupor and closed the jacket he'd donned earlier this morning. With resignation, he stepped out of the SUV, glaring at his guards when they glanced at him, then quickly turned away, looking down the street in both directions.

With a sigh of frustration and an enormous amount of self-discipline to get his body back under control, he turned and looked down at Faye. "Show me your paintings, Faye," he said, taking her hand and placing her fingers on the curve of his arm. It wasn't exactly the way he wanted her to touch him, but for the moment it was enough.

"This way," she said, leading him towards a steel security door that led directly into a warehouse like area. As she pulled out a plastic security keycard that allowed them entry, Faye explained what was going on, what was stored back here and why so many of the pieces of art and history weren't on display as she led him along a concrete floor and cinderblock wall area. Finally, they came to a larger room with long windows and another locked door. Faye put in the code and led him into what looked like a laboratory. "This is the restoration area," she explained. Briefly revealing her brilliance, she took him through the room, explaining what each of the pieces of equipment did.

Finally, they reached the restoration room where ten different paintings were leaning against the wall. There were several sticky notes on the table in front of each painting and Zantar thought about the map yesterday and all of the sticky notes he and the others had posted along the map. Seems as if people of all industries sometimes eschewed technology and went old-school with paper notes.

"This is where I work," she said with pride, her eyes sweeping over the notes and the paintings as if trying to assess where she should start. She dumped her bag on the floor, then grabbed his arm and pulled him down to the third painting from the end. "Look here," she said, pointing to a corner of the painting. "If you look at the overall painting, this is just an image of a man with the city in the background. But if you look down here at the left bottom corner, there's a compass right...here." She straightened and looked up at him, her eyes bright with curiosity. "Why is there a compass sitting on a table in the kitchen? And if you look out at the city," she turned to point out the window, "you can see smaller details such as this map attached to the wall. Why is there a map on a wall in the middle of the city?" she asked, handing him the magnifying glass.

Zantar bent over, examining the image. She was right. There was a map of the area somehow pinned to the wall of the city. What an odd thing to have added to a painting! Especially during the period in which the artist lived. At that point in history, maps were used mainly by the wealthy or on ocean vessels. And the maps that were around, they were rudimentary. But this one looked very detailed. Accurate? He didn't know.

"Is the map accurate?" he asked.

Faye looked up at him, startled by his question.

"I don't...I hadn't even thought about that! What an interesting question!" She hurried over to her stack of sticky notes and scribbled something down, slapping the note on the table in front of the painting.

For a long moment, Faye stared at the map, then the sticky note, then at the painting. It took her a moment before she remembered that Zantar was standing next to her. When she remembered, Faye looked up at him with a grimace. "Sorry. I tend to lose myself in these paintings and you brought up a very good question."

A moment later, Faye continued with her explanation of why this particular artist's paintings were so extraordinary.

"If you look over here," she said, once again grabbing his arm and tugging him down to the opposite end of the line of paintings. "This is just a picture of the ocean."

He stared at the picture, noting the swells of waves and the peaceful sunrise on the horizon. "Yes. It's a nice picture. Very calming."

She grinned. "Exactly! So if it's so calming, why is there a gardenia floating on the waves?" She lifted his hand that was still holding the magnifying glass so that it was right over the image of a flower that was indeed floating pointlessly on the waves. "And over here," she said, pointing to the opposite corner, "there is a strange box."

"I'd want to know what's in the box," he grumbled, moving his magnifying glass over so that he could examine the box. "The box is also decorated with gardenias."

She literally bounced with excitement. "You get it?" she gasped. "You see the mystery here?"

He straightened up, nodding slowly. "I get it," he said with an intense expression.

Faye tapped her chin with the pen she'd been holding. "I mean, it could simply be that the artist was bored with what he was painting and decided to put arbitrary objects in strange places."

"Or the artist could have been making a reference to something that he'd witnessed. Or it's a political statement. Or maybe, the map along the side of the wall is simply a map to his lover's house."

She turned her head slowly, her lips curling into a wide, open smile. "Exactly! There are so many possibilities!"

He laughed and pulled her into his arms. "It seems that you've chosen a fascinating artist to study."

She snuggled closer and Zantar couldn't deny how perfect she felt in his arms. The woman was making him crazy though. She was both innocent and sensual. Her movements against his chest were most likely simple excitement over her research. But every time she moved against him, it became harder and harder to hide his body's response. In the end, he stopped trying and simply lowered his head, kissing her as he'd wanted to do for the past several minutes.

Faye moaned when she felt his lips move and opened her mouth, wanting to deepen the kiss. Unconsciously, her hands slid up his chest and shoulders, her fingertips exploring the warm skin of his neck just above the dress shirt he wore before diving into his hair, pulling him even closer. She felt his hands on her hips, then lower, his big hands cupping her butt and pressing her body even closer.

When his hands lifted her higher, she gasped as the hard erection shifted against her core. Her fingers moved to his shoulders, bracing herself because the sensation was too intense. A moment later, she felt something behind but didn't realize that he'd lifted her up onto the table behind her. All she knew was that the hardness was right where she needed it.

Never in her life had she experienced desire this fast and this furious. She needed him. Faye needed him now! She wanted to rip his clothes off and wasn't even aware that they were in a room entirely made of windows where anyone from the warehouse area could look in and see them. All she was aware of was his mouth and his hands and that hardness pressing against her. She shifted again, her hands moving down from his shoulders, briefly exploring his chest before moving even lower. Her fingers gripped his butt and pulled him closer, moaning into his mouth as that hardness pressed against her even more intimately.

It was too much! She needed...something! "Zantar!" she whispered, her words a plea for help. She whimpered when he shifted against her and, if her eyes had been open, they might have rolled into the back of her head. Such was the pleasure and need that surged through her at that thrust. Every shift was like a bolt of electric current shooting straight to her core and her fingers curled into his butt, guiding him to exactly where she needed him to be.

Vaguely, she felt his hand slide under the knit top she'd donned earlier today. His fingers against the skin of her back, then her stomach before he finally cupped her breast. His touch was almost a distraction. Then his fingers slipped underneath her bra and...oh, dear heaven...he pinched her nipple. One of her hands moved to cover his, pressing his fingers, guiding them to do that pinching thing again. But he didn't! The dratted man simply slid his finger over her nipple and...oh, that felt really good too. Unfortunately, the sensation wasn't enough! It didn't give her what she needed. So she used her fingers to guide him, pressing against the rock hard globes of his butt as she lifted her hips higher, gasping every time he shifted against her.

Then he did it. He pinched her nipple again. And that was all it took! Faye's body exploded and she shivered as her body climaxed. Holding very still while waves of pleasure rolled over her, she kept her eyes closed while Zantar teased her neck. She could barely breathe, the pleasure was so intense and she shifted once again, reveling in the aftershocks.

When it was all over, she sighed, her body going limp against his big, wonderfully hard chest and she laid her head against his shoulder. "Oh my!" was all she could say.

The deep rumbling laughter as well as the fingers massaging her scalp brought her back to the present. Slowly, she forced her eyelids open and she looked up at the man who had magic fingers and a magic...!

"What...what just happened?" she whispered, pulling away and looking around. Thankfully, there were no other museum employees present at the moment. Plus, his big, tall body seemed to be shielding her from the windows on the opposite side of the room. But still, she'd just...climaxed! Even now, her body seemed to be humming with happiness and delicious sensations!

"You are beautiful, Faye!" he growled, his hands sliding up and down over her back in a soothing motion as he held her against his chest.

"I didn't just...!"

"You did," he corrected with a deep, sexy chuckle. "And it was amazing to hold you while you enjoyed your pleasure." He pulled away slightly, just enough to kiss her lips. "I eagerly anticipate enjoying that pleasure with you next time."

Faye pulled out of his arms and pushed herself off of the table. Thankfully, Zantar grabbed her upper arms, holding her steady when her legs almost gave out underneath her. But his hands were strong, and he waited until she nodded. "I'm okay," she whispered, smiling weakly up at him.

"You are more than okay, Faye," he said as he took her hand, lifting it up to his lips so that he could kiss her fingertips. "Please don't be embarrassed by what just happened," he urged when he saw the blush staining her cheeks. "It was beautiful and proved that you are a sensuous, lovely woman."

"I…can't believe that happened here! In the restoration room!" she whispered, once again looking around. "I really hope that there aren't any security cameras around here."

He laughed, then pulled her close again, hugging her. But he made a mental note to assign one of his guards to review the security footage, erasing anything that could be compromising. "Don't worry about that," he assured her.

She pressed her face against his chest, shaking her head. "That was so unprofessional of me!"

"It was glorious, Faye." He kissed the top of her head. "But I will leave here and allow you privacy so that you can continue your research. I look forward to speaking with you tonight and hearing what other symbols you have discovered today." With that, he stepped back and took her hand, once again kissing her fingers. "Thank you for showing me your work."

Faye watched as he turned and walked out of the restoration room, not revealing even a hint of what had transpired here. Thank goodness, she thought and leaned against the table as her legs began to tremble once more.

Turning, she tried to focus on the paintings. But it took her another fifteen minutes before her brain would start functioning again.

Taking a long drag on his cigarette, Scott leaned against the wall of a building situated right across the street from the museum he'd followed Faye to yesterday. He was waiting for Faye to arrive, wondering why she came to this dreary place every day. He was also irritated that she hadn't arrived already. The heat was starting to become intense, and several people were looking at him as if he were doing something wrong by just standing here.

He wanted to leave, go find a place that was cool, maybe with a nice bottle of scotch. Unfortunately, he needed cash to tide him over until his next payment from old man Neville and, as he stood there, he wondered if Faye had some sort of connection to the museum director. Was she sleeping with the guy? Was that why she snuck in through the back door every day? She only stayed a couple of hours, so a lurid affair with the well-off buffoon would make sense. In the back of his mind, he thought about taking pictures of Faye with the old fart. From the little he's seen of the guy, the museum director was a balding, simpering, blathering old goat that was probably too into art to ever get laid. But then he remembered that Faye loved art too. Okay, so maybe Faye was enamored of someone who liked art just as much as she did!

Figured, he mentally grumbled, taking another long draw on his cigarette. He breathed in deeply, letting the smoke fill his lungs, holding it there for a long moment before slowly releasing it into the air. He almost laughed when a group of teenagers walked by at that exact moment, most of them getting a face-full of his expelled smoke. They all waved their hands in front of their faces, glaring at him as they hurried past, but none of them dared to speak to him.

Good! Maybe he was getting that badass aura that he'd been striving to achieve for so long! It was about time! He'd been stuck with a boyish look well after his high school years, which was why he'd grown a beard. Damn thing didn't grow very well, though, and it itched like crazy.

He wondered if he should just shave the damn thing off and...!

His attention was captured when a line of black SUVs drove up, coming to a halt right in front of the non-descript entrance he was trying to watch. Who the hell needed that many SUVs?

As soon as the question had finished forming in his mind, he straightened away from the building's wall, his eyes and mind alert as he watched...holy hell! His stepsister was moving out of the SUV and...! Scott's eyes bulged as he watched the bitch walk into the back entrance of the museum on the arm of none other than the freaking Sheik of Citran! Holy hell, what was she doing with that bastard? And why was the huge man looking down at her as if she'd cast some sort of spell over him? Was the idiot in love with Faye? She was such a sappy, pathetic woman! She was a freaking art teacher for freak's sake! Art! No one cared about art! It wasn't like it contributed to the world in any way. Pictures were fine enough to look at but other than that, they were pointless!

So what was going on? Why was Faye sucking up to the giant bastard?

Scott smiled as he suddenly realized what was going on! Faye always acted so pure and sweet, but he knew the truth. The bitch must be playing the guy! He had to be worth billions! So yeah, she had a pretty good situation going on now! Mentally, he just doubled the amount of money he was going to ask her for. And there was no way in hell he'd ever pay her back. Not when she had a sweet sugar daddy helping her out! Hell, she probably wouldn't even remember the measly amount he was going to get from her.

But as he waited for the rich, royal bastard to come out, something else occurred to him. If Faye was screwing the guy, which was most likely, then maybe Scott could use Faye to get the guy to sign the mining contract for Citran that the old man wanted so desperately. Neville was right of course. If they had a signed contract, signed by the freaking leader of the country, no less, then there wouldn't be a need for all of this sneaking around and digging only at night! Of course, the contract didn't need to specify exactly what they were actually mining for. Or where. Hell no! The terms of the contract were all vague, saying that the mining company was only "speculating" on potential mineral deposits. Anything specific meant that the country would demand a percentage of the profits and that wasn't something that Mr. Neville would allow, hence all of the secrecy and vague contract terms. Until they had the contract signed, Scott dealt with the crappy night shifts and forcing people out of their homes instead of just buying up the land like some companies did.

His mind whirling with ideas, he carefully made plans while he waited for the bastard to leave. He suspected that he'd have the same couple of hours wait, so he was startled when the tall brute stepped through the door less than twenty minutes after he'd entered.

Good grief, even the museum director had received a bit more time and attention from his lovely, tediously boring stepsister! And was that a guard that had been left behind?

Unfortunately, the big goon's presence off to the side of the building kept Scott from approaching Faye before she went off to do the nasty with the museum director. He'd have to be a bit more careful about approaching her now.

Scott tried to relax, once more leaning against the building.

Normally, Faye rushed out of the museum an hour or two after her arrival. But even after three hours, Faye still hadn't emerged through the back door. Scott waited another hour, the heat increasing along with his temper. Where the hell was she? Why wasn't she coming out after a couple of hours like normal?

Muttering under his breath and disgusted that he was now out of cigarettes, Scott walked away, thinking he'd just have to catch her before she got to the coffee shop tomorrow morning. There was no way he was standing out here in this heat for who knew how long. He shook his head, wondering how Faye could do two men in the same morning. Well, the first guy had been pretty quick. Faye must have had plenty of time to work on the older guy after the sheik dude had left.

He chuckled, shaking his head at Faye's pathetic pretense of being such an upstanding, wonderful teacher. Hell, if her school administration knew what she did in her time off, they wouldn't keep her on staff.

Just thinking about that made him tuck that little threat into the back of his mind. If she didn't share the bounty, he'd just have to give her a little taste of the ruthlessness he'd learned over the past few years working for that psycho Neville.

Chapter 8

Faye almost danced down the street as she walked away from the museum. It was lovely to have spent so many hours working on the mystery of all of those interesting symbols in Mr. Tismona's paintings. She was attacking the issue from a different angle now. She'd taken pictures of every symbol and would print them out to see if there was an overarching theme to them. So far, she'd been trying to understand them within the context of the individual paintings. But maybe the answer to all of the mysterious objects was bigger than the individual pieces. Maybe the whole collection was more important than just one painting!
It was a two mile walk back to her apartment but thankfully the sun was setting by that time of day. She would shower and change clothes before walking over to the hotel for dinner with Zantar. At the thought of going to the hotel, on a day when she was supposed to be on sick leave, her stomach tightened. What if she ran into her boss? Or even worse, the hotel manager? She didn't want to see either man right now. Maybe she should call Zantar and ask if they could go out for dinner.
Then thoughts of this morning came back to her mind. Not that they'd ever really been far from her consciousness, she admonished herself. In fact, what had transpired earlier today had been taunting her all day. She would think about the beautiful pleasure he'd given to her that morning and...well, then she'd be tormented by how he'd walked away without any of the pleasure she'd enjoyed! And yet, she didn't really know how to pleasure him in the same way. Did men do it that way? With their clothes on? She suspected that it would be a bit messy if... oh good grief, she mentally muttered to herself. She was being ridiculous!
But was she?

Faye stepped into her tiny shower, trying to banish all of those thoughts from her mind. Unfortunately, they refused to leave, popping up and making her whole body tingle with the hope of more tonight.

Another good reason for them to go to a restaurant instead of dining at the hotel tonight.

Yes, she'd just call him and suggest that really great Mexican restaurant she'd discovered recently. They had excellent guacamole and the fish tacos were truly delicious!

Turning off the water, she stepped out of the tiny shower, wrapping a towel around her nakedness. "What to wear," she whispered to herself as she padded barefoot to the small closet in her tiny bedroom. She was shifting the hangars, examining the pretty sundresses she'd brought with her when someone knocked on the door. Faye's eyes swiveled over to the door, her heart thudding in her chest. No one knew where she lived except for the hotel. Had her boss come to her apartment, angry with her for not coming in to work? But the doctor had said that she should take time off! And the manager! Yesterday, he'd told her to get out!

"Oh dear," she whispered, grabbing her bathrobe and pulling it on, tightening the belt. It wasn't an appropriate outfit to be fired in, but Faye didn't have time to pull on something different because there was another pounding on her door.

Faye hurried over and pulled it open, intending to tell whoever was on the other side of the door to give her a moment to put on more appropriate clothing. But when she opened the door, Faye's mouth fell open as she took in Zantar standing outside, looking huge and magnificent. And furious!

"I thought we were meeting in an hour!" she gasped, her hand reaching up to grip the open neckline of her bathrobe.

"Are you okay?" he demanded, stepping into the room and looking around. As soon as he took in the small, studio apartment, his eyes sharpened. "Is this where you've been living?"

Faye looked around, taking in the full size bed and small sofa. There was a tiny kitchen area, but basically, it was all one room. Except for the bathroom. She had done her best to make the whole space pretty with her limited time and budget.

"It's good enough for my purposes," she told him. "I know that it's small, but I'm not here very often. The bed is very comfort..." she stopped when his eyes latched onto the bed, then swiveled towards her. The heat there caused her breath to catch in her throat! She could feel his desire and an answering call bubbled up inside of her.

"You just showered?" he asked, his voice deeper now.

"Yes."

"And you aren't hurt?"

She blinked, shaking her head. "Is that why you are here early? To make sure I'm okay? Why would you think I was hurt?"

"Yes," he replied, nodding sharply. "Someone was watching the back door to the museum today. I suspect that they were waiting for you to come out. Unfortunately, we haven't been able to identify the person yet."

Her eyes widened even more with that news. "Watching...? Why would they be waiting for me?" A dark eyebrow lifted and she gasped. "You think someone from the hotel was waiting to...hurt me?"

He shrugged. "The thought crossed my mind."

Faye leaned against the wall, shock causing her body to run hot, then cold and she shivered. "But...I...!"

Zantar couldn't hold back any longer. She just looked so lost and hurt. He pulled her into his arms, holding her close and trying to offer her comfort. He lived with threats to his life all the time. It was just a part of his existence. But Faye...she wasn't used to someone trying to hurt her and he could feel her trembling as she tried to process what he was telling her.

"My guards are looking into the situation, Faye. We'll get to the bottom of it." His hands dove into her hair, the wet strands still soft and he tangled his fingers in the tresses. "I'll protect you!" he told her harshly.

She lifted her eyes up to his, tilting her head back. "But...why?" she sniffed. "And who? I mean, I'm just a schoolteacher. I'm not very important!"

His fingers tightened in her hair because he couldn't believe what she was telling him. How could she think that way? "You're important to me!"

And with that, he kissed her, his mouth moving over hers as if she were his last breath and he had to inhale all of her. Lifting her up, he cradled her in his arms, unaware of what he was doing. All he knew was that he had to show her, had to prove that she was important to him.

When he'd heard the news that someone had been waiting for her... some sleazy male with a spotty beard and cheap clothes, but with an expensive watch...he'd just about lost his mind. He'd left the meetings early, explaining to the others that his woman was in trouble. He hadn't waited around to see if they understood. All he knew was that he had to get to Faye, to see her and hold her and make sure that she was safe and whole.

Kissing her, touching her, feeling her respond reassured him that she was safe, but it wasn't enough. Plus, now that he'd started, he couldn't seem to stop. Nor could he convince himself that there was a reason to stop! She wasn't pushing him away, they weren't in a public place and she felt too damn good!

Blindly, he lifted her up and carried her to the bed, kissing her the whole time. He couldn't seem to stop! When her fingers reached up, touching his skin, he knew that he didn't have to hold back. He couldn't hold back! Not this time.

Laying her down on the bed, he whipped off his tie and jacket, then released several buttons on his shirt, opening the material. "Touch me, Faye," he urged, his voice rough with need. "I need to feel your hands on my skin." He didn't wait for her. He simply lifted her hand and pressed her fingers against his chest, then closed his eyes as he absorbed her touch. It was even better than what he'd imagined over the past several nights while dreaming about this.

Then her fingers moved, her other hand came up and her touch singed him! He was on fire and her touch was like more gasoline, burning him hotter!

He grumbled, the sound coming low in his chest, then he found himself lowering over her, sliding onto the tiny bed so that he could feel her against his whole body. He flipped off his shoes and came down next to her, pressing one knee between her legs so that he could shift against her. That's all he'd do, he vowed. Just like this morning, he'd give her pleasure and then they'd leave. He'd take her out to dinner in a public restaurant, then kiss her good night afterwards and walk away.

But that was before his mind registered that she was completely naked underneath the thin robe. When his hands moved around to pull her close, the robe was already sliding away, the neckline opening for him to see the soft, perfect breasts tipped with pretty, pale pink nipples. He had to taste one, to feel the tip against his tongue. His hand reached around to cup her bottom, to feel her breast in his other hand. They were perfect! So absolutely perfect. And when he kissed the tip, Faye gasped. She wiggled. She groaned. So he tasted the tip, teased it, wanting to give her as much pleasure as possible.

That's when she did that thrusting thing with her hips, pressing her core against him in a rhythmic pattern. That, in addition to her touch, her fingers sliding against his chest and, dear heaven, lower to brush lightly against his erection, he was lost. So damn lost! Vaguely, he was aware of her fingers fumbling with the buckle on his belt, but he needed more of those gasps and kept teasing her nipples. Just one more gasp, he told himself, then he'd pull back. Just one more! Moving to her other breast, he started to take that tip into his mouth, but then he felt her fingers on his shaft! Her bare fingers! Damn, she wrapped her fingers around him, tugging him, smoothing her whole hand against him, that soft thumb rubbing around the edge, over the top, then just under the tip and he felt like he was about to explode! Just from a woman's hand? No, not just any woman's hand. This was Faye's hand. This was Faye touching him!

And with that realization, plus her shifting movements, he felt her guide him closer to her and he followed blindly. When he pressed against that wet heat, he closed his eyes, trying to remember something. It was something important!

Faye wanted to scream! Instead, she bit his shoulder, shifting against him, desperate to feel him fill her. She couldn't believe how desperately she needed to feel him fill her, to have Zantar inside of her. She was positive that, if he didn't enter her this exact moment, she would go insane! Every cell in her body was vibrating, trembling with the need to feel him inside of her and the dratted man wasn't moving fast enough! She shifted, trying to figure out how to get him to do what she needed.

And then he was there! She felt him nudge against her opening and she almost whimpered with relief! Grasping his shoulders, she arched against him, silently begging him to fill her, to make her whole! Just once in her life, she needed to feel that, to ease the aching, desperate need inside of her created by this man's hands and mouth!

He pressed into her heat then, the passage smooth and ready for him. He was huge! His entry slowed only because she wasn't used to him and she wiggled, ignoring his groan or the way his hands gripped her then. She needed all of him and he was moving too slowly. "Now Zantar!" she whispered, shocked at the way her voice sounded so hoarse.

In the next moment, he slid into her heat, feeling him fill her and she held her breath, willing her mind to relax so that she could take all of him. He was definitely larger than she'd anticipated, but he felt too good! Too perfect!

Before she'd had a chance to adjust to his size, he pulled back and she almost punched him. She'd actually curled her fingers into a fist to do just that, but then he thrust back into her and she gasped, wrapping her legs around his waist. Blindly, she reached up, gripping his shoulders as he pulled out, then thrust again, the friction making her mind whirl with unexpected sensations. It was too much. It wasn't enough! Shifting, she rubbed her legs against him, trying to get him to move faster because words failed her in this moment.

Finally, he thrust into her more rapidly, every thrust shifting against that nub and making her body spiral higher and higher. She wasn't aware of the sound she was making or the way Zantar looked down at her with an intensity that he'd never experienced before. All she was aware of was the need inside of her and the way his body helped her satisfy that need until…!

She saw stars! Faye literally saw stars as her body convulsed with waves of pleasure! She couldn't breathe, couldn't move, could only hang onto Zantar with all of her strength as she let the waves of pleasure race through her. She felt him moving inside of her, every additional thrust creating more shivers of pleasure until she thought she might just pass out. Finally he stopped, collapsing down on top of her and she tried to wrap her arms around him, but she couldn't move. Every muscle inside of her was unresponsive as she melted into the mattress, absorbing his weight because the world was finally right and wonderful.

A long time later, she opened her eyes and smiled. He was still inside of her, still holding her close and Faye wanted to laugh. She must have given in to the desire because he lifted his head, bracing his weight on his forearms as he looked down at her. "What's so funny?" he asked, his voice still rough and sexy.

She shrugged, lifting one leg so that she could slide her inner thigh against his hip while her hands moved up and down his upper arms. "Nothing," she replied, then laughed again.

"Why are you laughing then?" he asked and pulled out of her, moving quickly to the bathroom to get a washcloth. He cleaned himself and Faye lifted up onto her elbows to watch him. She loved the way his back rippled with muscles and she was even more amused to realize that he was still wearing his pants. Looking down at herself, she gasped at how wanton she looked with her robe completely spread open and her naked body splayed out. Pulling the robe closed, she scooted higher up onto the bed, pushing a pillow behind her. She tied the belt of the robe tightly and looked over at him warily when he approached the bed with the washcloth.

"What are you going to do with that?" she asked.

He lifted an eyebrow. "I'm going to clean you," he told her. "I…" he sighed, shaking his head. "I forgot to use a condom."

Faye stared at him, not understanding what he meant. Why would he worry about using a condom? And then the words finally sunk into her pleasure-muddled mind. No condom. No condom!

"Oh!" was all she could say. It was as far as her mind went. She stared at him, suddenly understanding why she really needed that washcloth. She reached for it, but he shook his head, pulling the cloth away as he put a hand on her knees. "I can do that," she told him frantically, shifting further away from him.

"I am sorry, Faye," he said, his fingers sliding along her calf gently. "Let me clean you up."

Faye looked at him, startled by the grim expression in his eyes. "You're upset?"

"Yes," he replied gruffly, his fingers wrapping around her ankle and tugging. "I was irresponsible, Faye."

"I was too," she whispered, her mind whirling with the potential problems.

"When was your last period?"

Her cheeks turned bright red with that question, and she reached out, taking the damp cloth from him. "Um..." she thought back. "I'm not sure. I'll have to look at the calendar on my phone." She still didn't clean herself up, too embarrassed to do that in front of him. Instead, she climbed off of the bed and walked into the bathroom, needing a moment of privacy.

Once the door was firmly, she closed her eyes and leaned against the wall. Unfortunately, the stickiness between her legs started to bother her and she frantically wiped away the evidence of her stupidity. Yes, Zantar blamed himself, but she was the one who would have to deal with the consequences of their actions. He could go on his merry way! He could go back to wherever he was from and continue on with his life!

Faye counted back the days, trying to remember when she'd last had her period, but her cycles weren't very consistent. Sometimes, she'd have a period in twenty-eight days and sometimes the next cycle would come in twenty days. Or even forty! She liked those times, getting a bit of extra time in between the cramps and the tedium of dealing with that time of the month. She didn't get mood swings or cravings like some women, but she definitely felt the cramps.

Sighing, she tossed the washcloth into the laundry basket, bracing her hands on the sink as she tried to process this situation.

A knock on the bathroom door startled her and she stood up, not sure how she could face Zantar again.

"Faye?" he called out through the door. "Are you okay?"

"I'm fine!" she lied. She wasn't fine. She was freaking out! And she was berating herself for being so out of control that she hadn't reminded, or more like demanded, that he use a condom!

"No, you're not," he countered, his voice barely muffed through the thin, cheap door.

She almost laughed but straightened up and pulled open the door, holding onto the doorknob as if it were a lifeline. Slowly, she let her eyes lift to his. "No. I'm not," she agreed with a very soft tilt of her head. "I'm sort of freaking out right now."

He nodded, then pulled her into his arms. He'd pulled his shirt back on and she laid her head against his chest, wishing that she could feel his skin again. She'd really liked that. Granted, there'd been a lot of aspects of the past...however long it had been since he'd stepped into her apartment...that she'd liked. No, loved. Yes, she'd loved making love with Zantar. He probably thought of their time together as just sex, but she...loved him. Yes, she truly loved him.

Love after only a few days? Was that possible?

No! Surely she didn't know the man well enough to be in love with him.

It was just a dopamine rush. New relationships always created a hazy, wonderful rush of dopamine and other "feel good" drugs that mimicked the sensation of being in love. But once they got to know each other better, she'd find things about the man that would irritate her.

For the moment, though, she needed his arms around her. She needed to feel his heartbeat, to know that he was here with her.

"I'm sorry," he said again, and he tightened his arms around her.

"I'm sorry too," she told him, pulling back slightly to look up at him. "I should have stopped us."

He shook his head. "No, I should have remembered." He lifted a hand, cupping the back of her head. "Think hard, love. When was your last period?"

Once again, she blushed, not used to sharing those kinds of details with a man. Not even the two boyfriends she'd had prior to now had asked her that question. She'd simply told them no whenever they'd started to kiss her and they'd understood that she was on her period and backed off. Of course, the sex hadn't ever been mind-blowing like it had been with Zantar. Before Zantar, sex...it had been something she'd done simply because she'd felt it was expected of her. But there hadn't ever been any pleasure in it for her. It was just part of a relationship. An annoying part – but she hadn't minded because Faye had enjoyed the snuggling after the fact.

"What are you thinking?" he asked, his thumb caressing her cheek softly. Tenderly.

She smiled, leaning into his touch. "I'm thinking that I finally understand what sex is all about," she admitted.

He looked startled and Faye smiled, shrugging lightly. "Sex wasn't like this with anyone else, Zantar."

"What was it like?"

She cringed. "Before you, it was…well, a chore, I guess is the best way to describe it." She smiled slightly at his stunned expression. "I would have sex in order to get to the good stuff."

He lifted an eyebrow. "What's the good stuff?" he asked, leaning forward to kiss her forehead.

"The snuggling and talking afterwards." She smiled up at him. "This."

He laughed and pulled her closer. "Ah, love," he sighed and kissed the top of her head again. "The good stuff should be all of it. But I'll admit that the sex was pretty…" he paused, and Faye could feel him shaking his head. "It was extraordinary," he finally admitted. "I've never been so far gone that I would forget protection."

That warmed her heart and that love-sensation intensified inside of her. Just dopamine, she reminded herself, but she rubbed her cheek against his chest, loving the way he felt and the smell of the aftershave he used.

"Why don't you get dressed and I'll take you out to dinner?"

Faye laughed and reluctantly pulled out of his arms. "That sounds nice," she told him. "What should I wear?"

Zantar looked down at Faye's robe, seeing the taut nipples pressing against the thin material and refrained from telling her that she looked quite lovely just the way she was now. His body ached to make love to her again. Hell, he ached to just hold her like this. For the rest of her life, if she'd allow him. He wasn't much of a snuggler, but if Faye liked to snuggle, he'd learn to snuggle with her. He wasn't even sure what that entailed, but he'd learn. He'd learn anything if it made her happy.

Her stomach rumbling broke through his musings, and he pulled away. "Dinner," he told her firmly, then turned to look at her wardrobe. It was painfully meager but perhaps that was simply because she'd traveled to Skyla with just what she could fit into a suitcase. He'd have to rectify her lack of an expansive wardrobe as well as learn to snuggle.

He reached into the closet and pulled out something red. When he held it up to examine the clothing, he realized that it was a pretty sundress. He held it out in front of her, then nodded. "Wear this," he told her, then bent down to examine her shoes. There wasn't really anything there that would match the dress and he made a mental note to ensure that shoes were purchased for all of the outfits he would get for her. He'd hire a professional dresser, someone who could look at Faye and understand both her taste and her body type so that the person would find outfits that Faye would feel comfortable and pretty wearing.

"I've only worn this once," she replied, lifting the dress from the hanger and tossing it over her shoulder. "I'll be right back."

"You're going into the bathroom to change?" he asked, trying to hide his amusement. "You know that I'm going to strip that off of you later tonight and see everything you're trying to hide from me, right?"

Faye stopped, bit her lower lip as she looked up at him then sighed. "Give me time," she asked. "I'll get there."

Then she was gone, hiding in the bathroom to dress.

Zantar stared at the closed door, wondering if they had the time. How long would they have together? He was only here in Skyla for a couple more days. Then he had to travel back home to Citran.

Would she come with him? He'd put that question to her tonight, he thought as he turned to find his suit jacket. Maybe they should eat at the hotel tonight instead of going out to a restaurant. Looking at his jacket, it didn't look too bad, but it was obvious that it had been on the floor for a period of time. Mentally, he chuckled at the situation. Normally, he wouldn't give a damn what anyone thought. Wrinkled jacket and tie...the world could speculate. But tonight, he wanted to be alone with Faye. He suspected that they had some serious topics to discuss and it might be better if they were alone.

When the door to the bathroom opened up, he turned to look at Faye. She stepped out into the room, glancing around nervously and unable to look him in the eye. Tossing his jacket over onto the rumpled bed, he moved closer, taking her hands into his. "Faye, look at me."

He waited until she lifted those beautiful, wary eyes up to him. "We did nothing wrong." When she continued to look at him as if he were about to condemn her for something horrible, he pulled her closer. "We're two consenting adults, Faye. Both of us have a healthy sexual appetite." Although, his appetite seemed significantly "healthier" with Faye than with any other woman. Even now, feeling her soft breasts press against his chest, he wanted to make love to her again.

"Yes, but normally my appetite isn't nearly so..." she glanced up at him, "voracious."

He stared at her then threw back his head, laughing with delight at her word usage. Pulling her close, he kissed the top of her head. "We'll figure this out, *habib*," he promised, then stepped back before his body burned too hot for her. Taking her hand, he grabbed his jacket and tie and, not bothering to put them back on, he led Faye out of the small apartment. Glancing over his shoulder, he vowed that the next time he made love to her, it would be on a bigger bed. One that was a hell of a lot more comfortable than her pathetic excuse for a sleeping surface.

Chapter 9

"I can't go in there!" Faye hissed when his driver pulled into the parking garage of the Ambassador Hotel. "I'm supposed to be on sick leave, remember?"

Zantar glanced over at the hotel doorway, then down at Faye. She seemed genuinely upset at the thought of walking into the hotel. He wanted to reassure her that she wouldn't be judged or condemned by the employees here. But was that correct? How would he view a staff member who called in sick, only to show up for a party? Which was essentially what Faye was doing.

"There is a private entrance and elevator," he promised. "You won't be seen."

"Yes, but the penthouse staff will see me!" she told him.

He hadn't thought of that. His memory flashed back to the previous day, when he'd snapped at the butler in the presence of the hotel general manager. Thinking quickly, he agreed that he was putting her into an awkward situation by bringing her here. He took her hands and said, "Love, I know that this is going to feel odd, but we have some issues we need to talk over. I don't want to take you to a restaurant for fear that a reporter might overhear our conversation. If I promise to protect our privacy, will you trust me?"

She considered his words for a long moment, then nodded. "Yes. I trust you."

The relief that surged through him with her assurance was strange. But also empowering! Because of her trust, he vowed to make sure that the penthouse staff were gone from the area before he brought her up. They could order room service and act as their own wait staff. No need for hotel employees to see Faye for any reason. Hell, maybe he should just move to a different hotel, so that they didn't need to worry about these issues.

Making that decision, he nodded and stepped out of the SUV, then reached in to take her hand. "I'll have my guards go up first and clear the way. They can then go down to the kitchens and get our dinner. Will that suffice?"

"That would be very nice," she replied, but then hesitated. "Am I putting too much of a burden on your staff by being silly?" she asked, glancing over to one of the guards. "I'm so sorry! I'm being insensitive!"

"This plan would actually be easier for us, ma'am," the guard assured her with a polite smile. "Fewer people to oversee."

Her mouth fell open with that assurance, but she rallied quickly, nodding her understanding. "Well, then I appreciate your help," she told the man, smiling shyly at him.

The man nodded and Zantar growled, taking her hand and placing it on his arm. "Stop flirting with my guards," he warned her.

Faye laughed, assuming that he was only teasing her. "Don't be ridiculous," she said, leaning her head against his shoulder. "You know that I only have eyes for you."

They waited for five minutes before the advanced guards texted that the penthouse had been cleared of all hotel employees.

Dinner that night was wonderful, although Faye couldn't remember what they'd eaten. As soon as they'd stepped into the penthouse, Zantar had handed her a menu while stripping off his shirt. "Can you order us something for dinner while I change?" he asked.

Faye might have nodded, but she wasn't sure. All she could do was watch him move up the stairs to the bedroom. When he came back downstairs moments later, wearing a pair of casual slacks and an open necked linen shirt, he looked magnificent.

"You're staring at me as if you'd rather eat me," he teased, taking her into his arms and kissing her. When he lifted his head to look down at her, they were both breathing heavily. "Would you like some wine? Maybe some champagne?"

Faye thought about the previous hour. Had it only been an hour ago that he'd given her the most intense pleasure? Surely it had been days ago. Because right now, her body didn't want food. It wanted him! She wanted him to take her into his arms and make love to her all over again. But slower this time. This time she wanted to explore him.

So was it her fault when her eyes dropped to his chest? They were alone. He was gorgeous and she was hungry. For him!

With a growl, he pulled her right back into his arms and kissed her. How they ended up in his bedroom, naked and panting as they both touched each other with hands and mouths, she wasn't sure. All she knew was that his mouth covered hers, his hands cupped her breasts while his thumbs rubbed her nipples. She might have screamed, but his mouth kissing hers absorbed any shock at his touch. She arched into him, her body on fire once again and she wanted to scream with frustration because she couldn't get him to enter her.

  Finally, too frustrated to ask anymore, she pushed him against the mattress, then straddled him. She wasn't exactly sure what to do here because he was so much larger than her two previous lovers, but she looked down at him, unaware of her hair flying every which way or her eyes devouring him. All she knew was that she wanted this man. She wanted to know everything about him. Kissing his chest, she tasted with her tongue, explored with her fingers and nibbled with her teeth in places she hoped he might like. When she reached that fascinating erection, her mouth hovered over him, her mind anticipating taking him into her mouth and tasting the essence of this powerful man. When she didn't immediately take him into her mouth, he lifted his head up, his neck muscles straining.

  The look in his eyes gave her a sense of power.

  "You think so?" he growled, starting to pull her higher and do...well, whatever it was that he wanted to do to her. But before he could overpower her, she took him in her mouth and he went rigid for a brief moment before his head finally fell back onto the mattress. He groaned, his hands diving into her hair, tangling in the dark tresses as she moved her mouth up and down over that shaft. She was thorough and eager, trying to bring him to the brink just like what had happened earlier tonight.

  Before long, Zantar growled and flipped their positions, grabbing her hands and lifting them up over her head. "Retribution soon!" he warned her as he slid into her heat. For a long moment, they savored the sensation of their bodies melding together. But then Zantar pulled out with a muttered curse and, leaning over to yank the bedside table open, he grabbed a condom. Ripping open the package, he rolled it down over his shaft.

  "Now let's try this again!" he said.

  Before Faye had a chance to be shocked at the second lack of sanity that could have consequences, he was thrusting into her, her body shifting, wiggling and arching into his thrusts. He just felt so good and then...then it wasn't good! It wasn't enough and she grabbed him, shifting against him in an effort to find that relief. When it came, the sensations seemed to rip through her, drenching her in pleasure so powerful, it was almost painful and she simply held onto Zantar as he found his own release. Moments later, they tumbled together, arms and limbs tangled as they dragged precious air into their lungs.

When they finally ate dinner, it was a buffet of desserts that Zantar insisted on feeding to Faye. And in the end, he ate most of the whipped cream off of her body, starting the craziness all over again.

Chapter 10

Faye was literally dancing down the street. The hotel had sent her a message letting her know that they would pay her for her sick leave, just as Zantar had promised. Even better, they'd let her know that she was on the schedule for the week following the end of her sick leave!

So she had money in the bank and could pay her rent, plus buy food for the next month. But even better, she now knew that she was madly in love with Zantar. They'd spent the past few nights together, talking, making love, eating, drinking, and just getting to know one another.

During the daylight hours, Faye had gone to the museum or library to research her artist and he'd gone to some mysterious meetings. But she'd meet back up with him at the end of her day and…normally, he'd take her into his arms to make love to her as soon as she stepped out of the private elevator. But sometimes, he'd just hold her and ask her about her day, about whatever she'd discovered during her hours of research, and they'd brainstorm about the issue. Initially, she'd asked what he'd done during his long meetings. After the first time she'd asked, he'd explained that his conversations during the day were top secret and he couldn't discuss them. So instead, Faye had simply asked if he was okay, how he was feeling and if there'd been any arguments during the conversations. That last question was prompted by the tension she could see in his eyes and in the tight muscles around his mouth. But he merely grimaced and pulled her closer, kissing her as if that would distract her.

It didn't. And his lack of an answer hurt her. He didn't trust her, and she understood, sort of, the secretive nature of whatever it was that he did. Briefly, she'd wondered if he was involved in something illegal and that was why he didn't want to tell her what he did during the day. But Faye was starting to understand him. And with that understanding came the knowledge that he was a deeply ethical person. He wouldn't be involved in anything illegal or unethical.

She wondered if he was somehow protecting her. That would make sense, she thought, turning the corner towards the museum. He was very protective, and Faye had laughed softly when he'd ordered her to move into the penthouse with him.

"No way," she'd laughed. "Could you imagine what my co-workers might say when I start back to work next week? I mean, I'd commute to the employee locker room via the super-secret private elevator in order to don my housekeeping uniform!" She'd shaken her head at that scenario. "No. That definitely wouldn't be a good option."

She smiled, thinking about his grimace as well as his arguments that he would fund her research so she could stop working at the hotel.

"Faye!" a male voice called out.

At first, she didn't hear it. Her mind was thinking about what she would do once Zantar had to leave at the end of the week. Every time she thought about him not being here, not seeing him every day, her heart ached and tears threatened.

"Faye!"

Startled, she stopped and turned, looking for whoever was calling her.

"Scott?" She turned and waited for him to catch up with her. He didn't look good, she thought. His face appeared bloated and there were dark circles under his eyes. His clothes were rumpled and, when he pulled up beside her, he smelled strange. Almost as if he hadn't showered or changed clothes in a few days. "Are you okay?"

He laughed, the sound coming out harsh and almost hysterical. "I will be," he told her, taking her arm in a hard grip. "I noticed that you are dating someone new."

Faye reared back, startled by his comment as well as the biting grip on her arm. She jerked her arm away, glaring up at him. "Are you stalking me, Scott?"

He laughed that frightening laugh again, nodding. "Yeah. I am."

She took a step back from him, stunned by his response. "Why?"

"Because I need your help."

She shook her head, suddenly wary. Scott hadn't ever been a very nice person. But now...something was very off about him. "How can I help you?"

"First of all, I need cash."

Faye's anger eased a bit as she reached into her cotton bag for her wallet. Scott wasn't her favorite person, but she could spare a bit of cash for him. "Will ten dollars be enough?" she asked. This loan...uh...gift, because she knew Scott would never pay her back...would hurt her food budget for the week, but she could spare it for him. She hadn't been getting her cup of coffee every morning, so she had a bit to spare. Plus, she was eating most dinners with Zantar, which saved her a great deal of money.

Scott grabbed her wallet and took out all of the cash, scowling down at the bills in his hand. "Only fifteen dollars?" he snarled. "Seriously? I need more than this!"

Faye jerked back again, terrified of this man. "Scott, what's going on?" she asked, trying to soothe him, at least until she could get away from him. She put a hand on his shoulder. "I don't have a lot of money until I get paid this Friday but – "

"You're dating a rich bastard! Get me some money!"

Faye heard Scott's words, but she couldn't understand them for a long moment. Then she blinked. "You really have been stalking me, haven't you?"

"Yes!" he growled, leaning forward until he was almost touching her nose with his own. His breath was rancid and Faye turned her head, closing her eyes as she tried not to gag.

When she had her stomach back under control, she turned and looked at him steadily. He was nearly the same height as she was, so Scott wasn't as intimidating as Zantar could be. "Scott, I have to go now. I have work to do."

She started walking again, determined to ignore her stepbrother. But he followed her, crowding her and almost causing her to trip over his feet when he suddenly stepped in front of her.

"Are you seriously going to tell me that the man isn't giving you loads of cash?" His laugh was brittle. "And what about the guy at the museum? You're banging him too! I'm sure he'd give you some money if you'd just ask prettily enough." He sneered and lowered his head again. "Or if you asked at the right time!"

Faye cringed away from him, horrified by his suggestion. "You're disgusting!" And she stepped around him, determined to get to the museum. She wanted to get away from Scott. He'd always been a bit crude, but never like this!

Immediately, he blocked her escape. "No, I'm furious that you've got yourself a sugar daddy, two sugar daddies, actually. And you're not willing to help me out!"

"You're a big boy," she snapped, pushing around him as she lowered her head in an effort to get to the museum. "Figure it out yourself!"

"Is everything okay, ma'am?" a different male voice asked.

Faye turned and looked at a tall stranger. He'd spoken in Arabic and had the kind of military posture that warned he meant business.

"I'm fine!" she whispered, stepping back again.

"Is this man bothering you?" the stranger asked.

Faye looked over at Scott, who was also staring at the man. When she glanced back at the scary guy, she shook her head. "No, he was just leaving." She looked over at Scott, silently warning him to get away from her.

Scott hesitated, evaluating his chances. But this tall stranger was big and looked intimidating enough that Scott backed down. "Talk to ya later, Faye!" Scott called out, pretending as if he weren't upset about anything at all as he sauntered away, sliding his hands into his pockets.

Faye let out the breath she hadn't realized she'd been holding. When Scott finally disappeared around the corner, she turned and smiled politely at the man. "Thank you for your help, sir," she told him.

"It was my pleasure," the man replied, tilted his head in greeting, then walked in the opposite direction.

Faye breathed in deeply, trying to calm her racing heart. Scott had always been a bit slimy, but he'd never accosted her before. What in the world was going on in with him now?

Dismissing the creep from her mind, she turned and headed towards the museum, hurrying now. She didn't want to be caught alone with Scott again. She made a mental note to take a different route back to her apartment tonight. And maybe she should avoid meeting Zantar tonight. If Scott knew about Zantar, which he obviously did since the slime ball had said something about her "sugar daddy", then she didn't want to give Scott any reason to harass Zantar.

"Are you alright?" Mr. Latro asked as soon as Faye pushed through the back door to the museum.

Faye stopped and sighed, trying to pull herself together. "Yes," she replied, smiling to the kind, older man. "I just ran into my step-brother. He was a bit...rude," she finished lamely.

Mr. Latro's eyes widened. "That's not good! Family should protect each other!"

Faye's smile was one sided this time. "Yes, well, he was older than me and already off to college by the time my mother married his father. We didn't really get to know each other very well during holidays and his class breaks."

They talked about her research after that and Faye explained her latest theory, which was that the symbols were tied together. She'd come up with a storyline for them, but wasn't willing to reveal everything to the man just yet, needing to research a few more historical events. She'd give him more details as well as a copy of her dissertation after she'd finished it. But Faye was pretty excited about her hypothesis. She even had old letters for primary sources from that time period to back up her theory. The discovery of the letters in Skyla's national library were key to solving some of the symbolism riddles and she was eager to find more letters. The letters were from government officials during that time period and reference places and events, political controversies, but even more importantly, they contained more than a little gossip. It was going to take longer than she'd anticipated, but the letters were key. She just…Faye had a limited amount of time here in Skyla. She had to figure out how to scan as many letters as she could so that she could read them later, once she was back in Georgia.

Faye spent several hours researching the symbols and scanning various letters, documenting her sources and asking both the museum director and library personnel for more information. The library was only two blocks away from the museum, so it was easy to walk between the two buildings during the day.

The library was also very technologically advanced, giving her access to the letters that normally would be kept in a water-tight, humidity and heat proofed storage unit. Thank goodness for digital files, she thought as she looked over her collection of letters. Otherwise, she'd be lugging boxes all over the place with the amount of information she was compiling!

Scott leaned his back against the wall, sipping his whiskey-laced coffee as he watched the workers heading down into the tunnels for the night. In six hours, the trucks would pull out, filled with the mineral deposits that would then head over to the processing center. He'd done this, he thought, trying to feel a sense of pride over his accomplishments. He'd hired all of these thugs and gotten this process up and running.

Then his thoughts turned to Faye. She'd looked lovely earlier today. But she was such a stubborn bitch! Always had been. Plus, she was snooty, thinking that she was better than everyone. He hadn't missed how she'd sneered at him.

Granted, he smelled pretty ripe these days. But Faye didn't know how hard he'd been working. Plus, he didn't have the money for a hotel until he got his next payment installment, which wouldn't happen until… he wasn't sure. The mining operation might be ahead of schedule, but his payments were based off of mineral loads, not time.

Another truck filled with dirt and efiasia rumbled out of the tunnel, heading towards the processing plant on the other side of the border. Another motherload, he thought as he noticed the yellowish tinge to the dirt. Yellow indicated a heavy efiasia vein had been hit. Good!

Surely, that was enough to get old Neville off his back!

His phone rang and Scott pulled it out of his pocket, groaning as he read who the caller was. "Speak of the devil," he muttered, lifting the phone to his ear. "Mr. Neville! How can I help you?"

"Did you get the contracts signed?" the man asked, not bothering with niceties. Hell, he was rich enough not to need to bother!

"Not yet," Scott replied. "I'm still working on that. But I'll…"

"You have twenty-four hours." The line went dead after the bastard issued that new deadline.

Scott stared at the phone, his mind reeling with fear. Twenty-four hours to get fake contracts signed by the leader of the freaking country? Or what? Maybe it was worse not to know what his fate was. That way, his mind started to imagine the worst.

Scott leaned his head back, closing his eyes as the intense sun beat down on him. He needed a shower, but in order to get a shower, he needed money! That stupid prostitute had stolen all of his cash! Damn her! If he ever saw her again, she was going to pay with her flesh!

The last four words stuck in his mind, and he thought about them. "Hmmm!"

He pushed away from the wall, a plan forming in his mind. Maybe there was a way for him to get what he needed after all!

Chapter 11

"Hi!" Faye called out, stepping into the cool penthouse. But her eyes locked with Zantar's and instantly, she was wary. His eyes were bright with anger, his hands fisted on his lean hips. But it was the tension in his shoulders that warned him that his mood was dangerous.

"Who accosted you earlier today?" Zantar demanded.

Faye instantly relaxed. She'd actually forgotten about Scott's "visit" on the sidewalk outside of the museum earlier today.

"Oh, that was just my step-brother," she sighed, letting her cotton bag drop to the marble floor near the doorway, careful since the bag contained her laptop. She brought it with her everywhere now, too concerned about someone stealing it if she left it at the small apartment. The locks weren't great, and it felt as if her whole life was on that hard drive.

"He touched you!" Zantar snarled, lifting her arm, his teeth clenching.

Faye looked down at her arm, surprised to see the bruises there. "Oh," she whispered, startled. "Yeah. He was...upset about something."

"And he took money from you."

How in the world had he discovered that information? "Yes." She bit her lip, not sure how to dismiss that. "Well, I was going to give him some and..."

"And he took the rest," Zantar finished for her. "You were robbed, Faye!"

Faye looked around, startled to find several of Zantar's guards standing around, including one man who looked vaguely familiar! "You!" she gasped, stepping away from Zantar. "That's the man who stopped Scott from....!" It was the man from the sidewalk! She suddenly realized what was going on and knew she needed to ease the tension. Not just in Zantar, but in all of the men. "You don't need to worry about

Scott," she lied. Even she'd been concerned this morning. But they didn't need to know that. "He wasn't going to hurt me."

"And yet, he did hurt you!" Zantar countered. She heard a few of his guards' grunt their agreement and all of them looked ready to go out and find Scott so they could dismember him.

She waved the bruises on her arm away. She hadn't even realized that they were there until he'd pointed them out to her a moment ago. "This is nothing," she said again. "Why did you have me followed? Do you not trust me?"

Zantar's eyes widened in disbelief. "Trust you? I trust you more than I've ever trusted any woman, Faye," he replied, his voice softening. "Just the opposite. I think you are too trusting which is why I had my men looking out for you. It wasn't because I don't trust you, *habib*," he said, cupping her face gently. "It's because you…you are important to me."

Faye was stunned by that revelation and, for a long moment, she simply stared up at him, her heart thudding against her ribs. Then that same heart melted with his words as the love she'd felt growing inside of her burst into a beautiful spiral of fireworks, heating her from the inside. It wasn't a declaration of his love for her. But it was close enough. It wasn't nearly the same way she felt about him, but…! Well, it would be enough for now, she told herself.

"I care for you too," she whispered, then glanced around, not wanting to admit her feelings for Zantar with an audience. Thankfully, the guards were sensitive enough to have disappeared. How such large men moved so silently, Faye had no idea. But now that they were alone, she focused all of her attention on Zantar. "You're a magnificent man, Zantar. And we only have," her voice cracked as emotion overwhelmed her. "We only have one more day together. You head back to Citran and I…!" She closed her eyes, leaning her cheek against his chest as he pulled her closer.

"I wanted to talk to you about that," he said, not waiting for her to finish. "I want you to come back to Citran with me."

She laughed, but it was a shaky sound. "You know I can't."

"You can."

"No, I have to finish my research," she told him firmly. She pulled back, remaining in his arms because she couldn't stand the thought of not touching him. "This is really important for me, Zantar. You know that. It's my future. If I don't get this research done, then I won't be able to submit my dissertation." She fisted his shirt in her hands, trying to get him to understand. "I'm so close! I think I have everything figured out. I just need a few more pieces to the puzzle and then I can write everything up and submit it to the panel for review." She implored him with her eyes. "Please, Zantar! I need you to understand how important this is to me."

He sighed and lowered his head to kiss her. "I understand," he replied. "But I want you to stay here in the penthouse while you finish."

Faye was so startled by his suggestion that she didn't have time to stifle her laugh. "No. That's not going to happen."

"Why not?"

"Because I'm not mooching off of you, Zantar. That's not what we're about."

His fingers tightened on her waist as he looked at her. "What are we about?"

Faye's heart thudded in her chest as she stared up into his dark eyes. "I don't know. This is all…it's so new. So strange." Her fingers unclenched his shirt and she slid her fingers over his chest. "I don't understand what's happening to me, Zantar. I've never felt like this about anyone before. You're on my mind all the time. And when I'm finished at the library or the museum, my first thought is that I want to tell you everything I've discovered."

"I like that about you," he replied, then bent down, lifting her into his arms.

Faye squeaked, then laughed as he carried her up the stairs. "What are you doing, you crazy man!" she laughed.

He grunted as he shouldered his way into the bedroom, kicking the door closed behind them. "If you don't know the answer to that by now, then I've been doing something wrong over the past few days," he told her as he tossed her into the middle of the bed. A moment later, he was stripping off his clothes. "I'm going to make love to you until you agree to stay here, Faye."

She came up onto her elbows, watching as his tanned skin appeared with each piece of clothing discarded. "Is that a challenge?" she asked softly, letting her eyes move over him.

"*Ah 'ajal!*" he murmured, lowering himself down over her.

"Oh yes!" Faye translated as she lifted her arms to wrap around his neck and her legs to wrap around his hips.

And that was the end of coherent thought as he kissed and touched and drove her out of her mind until she tried to take control. For a brief period, Faye was allowed to hover over him, kissing and tasting and driving him wild until he took control away from her, flipping Faye onto her back once more. He then pinned her hands over her head as he slid into her heat, making her gasp as she wiggled to adjust to his invasion.

"More," she whispered when he remained inside of her, not moving as he breathed in her arousal. "*Akthar!*" she repeated in Arabic, just in case he wasn't thinking clearly.

With that encouragement, he slowly began thrusting, pushing into her heat, making her body throb with the need for fulfillment. Which he didn't give her. Not until she was screaming and writhing underneath him, her fingernails clutching at his shoulders as she begged him. Only then did he give them what they both wanted, what they both needed!

When it was all over, Zantar held her gently in his arms, his hands stroking her back as he savored the sensation of her breath on his chest. She was leaving him, he thought. Tomorrow, he would fly back to Citran and she would stay here, continuing her research. And she'd start working as a housekeeper for the hotel. He didn't want that for her. Lifting one of her hands, he stared at the blisters that had finally healed. The scars were still visible on her hands and around her fingertips. This should never have happened. He'd mentioned the abuse to Astir, who had immediately started an investigation. But that wasn't enough. Yes, the current hotel employees would be compensated by the hotel for the chemical abuse. The employees' medical bills would be paid and the hotel management would be fined, painfully, for the use of unauthorized chemicals.

But Faye would still be here. She would still be protected since he would leave several men here to watch out for her. He would wait until she'd finished her dissertation. That was important to her. He understood that, but he didn't have to like it.

Once she'd received her doctoral designation, he'd somehow convince her to come to Citran. She was brilliant and beautiful, kind and compassionate. His people would love her! She'd fight for the little guy, he knew. She'd look into all of the horrible jobs, the tasks that the average person ignored because some poor, unfortunate soul did the dirty work. Faye would fight for their rights! Because of what she'd just been through, she'd be a powerful advocate for the people who didn't have a voice.

That was exactly what Citran needed, he thought. Plus, Zantar acknowledged that he needed Faye. With every breath, he knew that she was the woman he wanted by his side for the rest of his life.

So how was he going to keep her by his side?

For the moment, Zantar accepted that he needed to let her go. Just for now. Just for the next few weeks. However, he'd already arranged for Faye to receive a grant proposal from Skyla's government to study one of their under-valued, soon-to-be-famous artists. As soon as Astir had heard about Faye's research, he'd been interested in supporting her efforts. Now Faye just needed to accept the grant. It would cover her living expenses, so she just needed to finish her research.

Zantar figured that, if she didn't have to work at the hotel for eight or nine hours a day, she could spend more time at the library and museum, allowing her to finish her research faster.

It was a sound investment on both sides. Skyla would gain recognition for an artist that truly was a national treasure, and Faye would gain the international attention that she deserved after publishing her research. The museum director, Latros something or other, was going to present the grant money to her tomorrow as soon as she arrived at the museum.

She could focus on her research, and Zantar would get Faye to Citran faster!

Having worked that out in his mind, he closed his eyes, allowing himself to fall asleep for the night.

Chapter 12

Faye walked slowly down the sidewalk, taking a different route than yesterday. She suspected that Zantar's guards were following her, but she hadn't seen them so far.

Did she care? Not really. She'd said goodbye to him earlier today. He was flying home, he'd told her. But he expected to hear from her as soon as she'd finished her dissertation.

Yes, she anticipated sending him a copy of her dissertation. But was that enough? Not really. She wanted Zantar. She wanted to talk to him every night. She wanted to share her life with him, not simply send him her finished paper.

Wiping away the tears that spilled down over her lashes, Faye blinked and tried to focus on the sidewalk in front of her.

Maybe if she hadn't been crying, or perhaps if she hadn't been running late, or maybe if she'd gotten more sleep and wasn't feeling so horrible that morning, Faye might have seen Scott approach her as she turned the corner on a building.

But none of that happened and Scott came out of an alley, grabbed her arm and yanked her into the shadows to pin her against the wall. It all happened so fast, she doubted that the guards had even noticed!

"Listen here, little sis!" Scott snarled, pressing her back against the brick wall. "You're going to tell your boyfriend to sign a contract with Green Mining! Understand?"

Faye stared up at him, shocked at how his appearance had deteriorated just in the past twenty-four hours. Yesterday, he'd looked horrible. Today, he looked like someone had peed on him and lit a match to burn off whatever alcohol had been in the urine!

"I don't understand!" she gasped, trying to reach up and touch her head. He'd pushed her against the wall so hard that her head had slammed against the bricks, making her head throb with pain.

"Tell your boyfriend to sign the contract," he hissed, moving closer. His breath made her stomach roil, "Or I will release pictures of you with some of your little boy toy students!"

Faye's hand stilled, the pain forgotten as she grasped the meaning of his words. "I've never done anything to my male students!" she hissed, horrified by what he was asking. "I've never even been alone with a student, not in my classroom or anywhere!"

He laughed, shaking his head. "Probably not, because you're such a freaking prude! But ya know what? Technology is a wonderful thing, Faye! I can create pictures of you in the most compromising positions with as many males and," he paused, his eyes lighting with anticipation, "and female students. Trust me, I know internet sites where women are doing things that would make a whore blush! And with your pretty face plastered on top of those sites, along with a few of those pretty boys and girls from their Facebook pages...!" he snickered, nodding his head, "Yeah, I don't think that the school board will think their art teacher is the virtuous little priss-ass that you present to the world. Now what do you say? Play ball? Or will I have to get creative?"

Faye's whole body turned cold with the horror of his threat. Could he really do that? Could he produce pictures of her doing...things...with her students? Dear heaven, he probably could! Scott had always been less than ethical, but she had no doubt that he could sink that low! Yes, he'd actually take pleasure in sinking her reputation with the school system! And she could then say goodbye to any PhD designation!

She shivered as she pictured her entire future going straight to hell, just because Scott could make up stories and create pictures that would all be lies!

He pulled back, sneering down at her. "And if that threat doesn't convince you to help me out, think of your new boyfriend. He might be big, but I have ways to bring people down. A bullet in the head is a pretty easy way to remain outside of another's fists!" Scott laughed at the horror on her features and tightened his grip. "I have resources, Faye," he said with a snarling whisper. "I will shoot your boyfriend down the next time he gets out of his car. Or maybe I'll kidnap him, chain him up like a dog and torture him before I get rid of him!" He nodded as if to emphasize his threat, releasing her arms and stepping back. "Tell him to sign the contract, Faye!" He started to walk away. "Green Mining. He needs to sign the contract by tomorrow." He was nearly out of the alley when he called back, "And it would be best if he didn't read the contract terms before he signed. Do something to distract him!"

Then he was gone.

Faye stood in the alley, no longer smelling the rotting food or the other disgusting scents. All she could think about was Scott's threat. He could ruin her! He could destroy her future with just a few pictures. He didn't even need to create pictures with her own students. An image of her with any teenager would destroy her life! No school system would accept her, no college would even touch her with that kind of horrific accusation hanging over her head. Even if the pictures were proven to be lies, schools would treat her like a pariah! They'd assume the old "where there's smoke, there's fire" adage. Or they'd assume that she was involved with unsavory characters, like Scott, and not want to bring that danger close to themselves in case it followed her.

And the threat of him shooting Zantar? The thought of Zantar being tortured for any reason, even for a moment, made her bend over and throw up her breakfast. Even when her stomach was empty, the heaves continued as the horror of Zantar being hurt in any way kept flashing through her mind.

No, she couldn't allow Scott to hurt Zantar.

There was only one thing she could do!

Chapter 13

Faye didn't pace around. She didn't bite her nails or create horrific timelines in her mind. She sat on the sofa in the magnificent penthouse. Waiting.

"Ma'am, can I get you some coffee or tea? Perhaps a glass of wine while you wait?"

Faye looked up, surprised to discover that her neck was stiff. Wine? It was only…! She glanced at the time on her cell phone, startled to find that she'd been sitting on the sofa for two hours. Two hours! Goodness, she hadn't realized how late it was! Or perhaps she hadn't realized how early she'd arrived. It hadn't taken long for her to tell her boss that she'd have to quit her job.

"Perhaps something stronger?" the man suggested.

Faye blinked, not sure what he was talking about. Her mind was still on the miserable conversation she'd just had with…she glanced at the time again…that conversation with her boss had been a while ago.

Taking a deep breath, she shook her head. "No. No wine. I'm fine."

The man hesitated, then nodded and backed away. Alone again, Faye's mind drifted once more, flitting through the nights with Zantar. Today he was flying back to…well, she wasn't sure where he was flying back to. Had he mentioned where he lived? No. She suddenly realized that their conversations were about their likes and dislikes, books they'd read, movies they'd enjoyed and various topics of conversations, but not where each of them lived. Perhaps she'd mentioned that she lived in Georgia in the United States, but had she told him what city? Maybe if he didn't know, Scott didn't either! After graduating from college, Faye had moved far away from Texas, where her mother and stepfather lived. Maybe Scott's ignorance of Faye's hometown would keep Zantar safe as well! And maybe she could convince Zantar to go away, to hide from...from the despicable threats from her stepbrother.

She sighed, rubbing her forehead. It didn't matter how far Zantar traveled, Scott was vengeful. He would find Zantar. She would have to...!

The door to the penthouse opened and Faye stood up, vaguely aware that her knees were shaking now and her stomach felt sick.

"Be strong," she whispered.

"Faye?" Zantar called out, striding into the great room until his eyes found her. Faye stood there, waiting for him to come to her, trembling at what she'd have to do. It wasn't fair or ethical. She'd always prided herself on being both of those but now...now she'd have to...and it broke her heart. This was going to ruin any future she might have had with Zantar.

"What's wrong, *habib*?" he asked, coming to her and pulling her into his arms. "Tell me what's wrong!"

Faye shivered, fighting back tears as she pressed her cheek against his chest, listening to his heart beating. She wrapped her arms around his waist, pressing herself against the hard muscles of his body and enjoying this moment with his strong arms holding her tight.

But only a moment, she told herself, pulling back enough so that she could see into his eyes. Those dark, amazing eyes caused tears to well up inside of her. She wished this didn't have to happen. Faye wanted to love this man! And she did! But he could never love her back. Not after this! Damn Scott for making her do this! She hated her step brother! At this moment, she hated her mother for bringing Scott into her life and she hated Scott's father because Scott was such a horrible human being.

She hated...a lot of things right now.

Taking a deep breath, she closed her eyes, bracing her hands on his chest as she said, "Don't sign the Green Mining contract!" The words rushed out of her mouth before she could stop them. Before she could stop herself from selfishly saving her future. "I don't know what's going on with that company, but something is seriously wrong. Stay away from that company."

He looked down at her, his dark eyes confused and concerned. "What are you talking about? I've never heard of 'Green Mining' and I'm not signing any mining contracts right now." he explained, his hands tightening on her waist.

Faye shook her head. "I don't really know what's going on. But if you ever hear about Green Mining, don't sign the contract." She pulled back, relieved when Zantar released her waist but continued staring at her with confusion in his wonderful, dark eyes. "Green Mining," she said again with urgent emphasis. "Don't sign anything with them!" She took a step towards the exit, then stopped and turned back. "One more thing." She paused, taking a breath and then looked up at him. "I love you!"

And with that, she hurried out of the penthouse. She jabbed at the private elevator, needing the doors to close before she selfishly rushed back into his arms. But she couldn't! Faye knew that she couldn't stay here because Scott would use her to get to Zantar.

Faye could see that Zantar was too stunned to react initially and that was probably the only reason she made it to the elevator without him stopping her. But as she turned to face him once more, she could see the determination in his eyes the split second before the doors closed and the elevator started to descend.

That was all the control she could muster, and Faye burst into tears as the elevator took her down to the fifth floor. There, she got off and sent the elevator down to the garage level just as she stepped off. From her experience over the past few days, Faye knew that there was a guard stationed in the parking garage, ensuring that no one could use this particular elevator without their consent.

Walking down the hallway, she slipped into a room with her housekeeping key-card, grabbed her backpack, the only thing she'd allowed herself to carry for the next part of her journey, checked the front pocket to ensure that her passport and wallet were still there, then slung it over her shoulder as she walked down the hallway, leaving the housekeeping key card on the bureau. She wouldn't need that any longer. Not after today.

She took the stairs to the ground floor, stepped out into the early evening heat via a side door and…just walked. She didn't run, because she suspected that Scott was watching for her. She had no idea where he was, but whatever was going on with him, he was quite desperate. If he caught her leaving the city, he would know that she'd warned Zantar.

Faye had planned this out well. Stepping into a grocery store, she went straight to the back and pulled out a plain, dark scarf, flipping it over her hair and she donned a different jacket. Then she wove her way through the storage areas of the grocery store and came out through the loading docks. If Scott was watching her, he would still be waiting for her to come out through the front doors.

It took a half hour of walking, but she finally made it to the bus station just in time to jump onto the first bus that was leaving. Faye had no idea where it was going, nor did she care. Faye only knew that she had to get out of town. Out of Scott's reach. If he ever found her, then he'd ruin her! He might do that anyway, just for retribution. Sneaking away from him, Faye knew that he'd figure out that she hadn't convinced Zantar to sign that contract. But hopefully, he wouldn't figure it out for another couple days. By then, she'd be far away! If Scott actually manipulated pictures of her, then…well, it didn't matter anymore. She'd take the hit to her career as long as Zantar was safe.

Chapter 14

Zantar glared down at the shorter, dirtier man stepping through the doors to the conference room. He looked smug and overly confident.

"What is your relationship to Faye Lafayette?" Zantar demanded, crossing his arms over his chest as he glared at the disgusting man from across the table.

The other man stopped, startled by the abrupt question. The smug expression was still there, but his gaze wasn't nearly as confident. "Faye is my step sister," Scott explained. His lips curled into a sniveling expression. "Pretty girl. Not too bright though. She was working as a maid, but I suspect that she's supplemented her income in..." his smile turned even slimier as he paused, "other ways."

The man set the Green Mining contracts down on the table, and Zantar suspected that the slimy man thought that the topic of Faye was closed. Buffoon!

"First of all, she's not a girl. You will refer to her as a woman or a lady. Nothing else is appropriate." Zantar growled, then paused as he watched the short, pudgy man's eyes widened.

The guy blinked and the smug expression dissipated. "Yes. Yes, of course. I didn't mean to insult her. I know that you and she were..." a smarmy smile curled the corners of his mouth. "Well, you two were friends, right?"

Zantar slowly moved around the polished wood table, restraining himself from lifting the chairs and throwing them at the asshole. He hadn't seen Faye in three days! Three days during which not even his guards could find a trace of her! Zantar was livid that Faye had warned him against signing an agreement with this mysterious "Green Mining" company, then left before offering any other explanation. The only story that Zantar could come up with was that this man, her step brother, had threatened her in some way.

"Faye is more than just a friend to me," Zantar explained, his voice lowering to barely above a whisper. "What did you say to her?"

Scott pulled back, noticing a strange vibe. This meeting was supposed to be about this ass signing a contract with the shell company that old man Neville had created. Green Mining wasn't actually a business entity, it was merely a cover title that allowed Neville to shift funding around, hiding the illegal activities that the old bastard was doing around the world. On the surface, Green Mining was clean, Scott knew. It had this ridiculous web site that told the world how the workers used only environmentally safe mining methods that were cleaner for the world, safer for the workers, and cost more than other processes. The site even went so far as to say that twenty percent of the profits went to the community in which the company mined.

It was all bogus. The workers were paid, but because most of them were illegal workers from other countries, Neville paid them cash to avoid tax issues. Furthermore, those wages weren't even half of the minimum wage for whatever country Neville was pilfering.

In this particular case, Scott needed the Sheik of Citran to sign the contracts that would allow them to mine one area, allowing them to covertly dig tunnels in Citran that would connect the previously excavated mines in Skyla and Silar, and eventually even Minar. The countries bordered each other, but once these tunnels were finished, Neville could mine resources from one country and take them out in another country through these underground tunnels. Scott suspected that the tunnels would be used for other purposes, possibly drug trafficking or even human traffickers, but what did he care as long as he got paid?

Once Scott presented this contract to the old man, Neville had promised Scott a massive payout. This contract was the lynch pin that would make all of the other efforts easier!

"Faye is a lovely g…uh…woman," Scott replied, his mind trying to sift through the odd undercurrents of this meeting. Why was this bastard so worried about Faye? Hell, if the guy wanted a woman, there were plenty out there who would do.

"She's gone!" the man snapped.

Scott recognized the lethal menace in this man's voice and finally understood the issue. Faye was gone? Hmmm…that was a smart move on her part!

However, this was Scott's specialty, he thought and smiled, relieved that the problem was so easily resolved. "Look, if you're looking for a replacement, I know of this brothel where the owner allows the customers to do whatever they want." His smile widened as the Sheik's interest sharpened. "It's true!" he laughed. "The things this owner said I could do to the women...hell, I didn't even know some of those things were possible!"

"And the women enjoy these...activities?" the Sheik replied.

Scott was thinking about the last time he'd visited the brothel and the crazy few hours he'd enjoyed. His mind blurred for several seconds in remembered lust, otherwise he might have recognized the newly dangerous tone in the other man's voice. He chuckled, shaking his head at the insane memories. "The girls are so doped up, I don't think that any of them are even aware of what the customers are doing to them!" Scott explained, laughing as he shook his head. "It's actually a brilliant place."

"You have enjoyed the...entertainment...of these girls?" Sheik al Abbous asked, his voice now silky soft.

"Hell yes!" Scott laughed. He pulled a pen out of his jacket pocket and clicked the end. "How about if we sign these contracts and then we can go have some fun to celebrate. Let's get this business over with, then I'll take you there. You're going to love it! My treat!"

Scott watched as the man sat down on the edge of the table. "Tell me what...experiments you've enjoyed at this brothel. Which of these girls have you patronized so far?"

Scott chuckled, then sat down next to the man, feeling a camaraderie now that they were discussing his specialty; namely, women. This "sheik" dude wasn't nearly as intimidating as everyone thought. The guy was just like any other guy with a healthy dick. He wanted the pleasure that a decadent society could offer, and Scott was one who had sampled a great many lovely decadent flavors from this particular buffet.

"There's this one chick who..."

Scott regaled Zantar with tales of his exploits in this particular place that he called a brothel. It didn't sound like a brothel. It sounded like a prison where women were drugged and trafficked for pathetic men who didn't like their women sentient.

Zantar shifted in order to ensure that the hidden cameras got a good view of Scott Roland's confessions. Zantar had only wanted to get information that might help him find Faye. It had been too long since she'd walked out of the penthouse in Skyla with Faye on his arm. He missed her with every breath he took! He looked for her whenever he left the palace, praying that she'd somehow come to Citran and would come back into his life. But knowing that his hopes were unrealistic, that something had scared her and it was probably this man, Zantar had ordered his guards to find her and bring her to him. He'd keep her safe. If she didn't want to be with him, then he'd ensure her safety somewhere else, but he had to know that Faye was alive and safe. He had to!

She loved him. Damn her, why had she said those things and then left him? Why had she disappeared from his life? Didn't she know that he would protect her? With his own life if necessary!

He had to find her. His guards had some good leads, but so far, she'd kept ahead of their efforts. Every time they thought that perhaps they'd caught up with her, she slipped away again.

Zantar didn't do or say anything to halt this parasite's confession. The things that this man confessed to were illegal in so many ways! Zantar lifted an eyebrow at some of the things Scott Roland said. Zantar was disgusted, but Roland mistook that expression as encouragement and went into more details, laughing at his demented exploits!

After several more stories, Zantar lifted a hand, stopping him. "Enough," he finally said, interrupting Roland's sick stories. "That should be enough." He turned and looked down at the contract. "Is this a copy of what you emailed to my assistant yesterday?"

"Yep!" Roland replied, standing as well and bracing his hands on the top of the table. "It's all there. Green Mining is just looking for rights to use this road," he explained, flipping the pages to show a map. "We're trying to transport supplies from this agricultural area to the production lines here," he said, pointing to the area near the mountains where Zantar and his neighbors had discovered what was really happening. It wasn't just road usage, Zantar mentally corrected.

"What's happening with the villages here in Skyla?" Zantar asked, pointing to the map. "I heard that one entire village collapsed for some mysterious reason."

Roland nodded, feigning concern. "I heard about those cave-ins," he replied. "Very sad." He added a serious shake of his head, but Zantar kept silent. "My boss was also concerned about that issue and sent some of his engineers to investigate. Apparently, there were some pretty severe sinkholes under the village caused by excess water usage by the villagers." He sighed as if he were concerned about the villagers. "It's a shame, but we have several products that can lower the water usage in residential areas. I can recommend a few of them myself."

"That's very generous of you," Zantar commented. "It's my understanding that Sheik del Taran also sent some specialists to that area and discovered an illegal mine that tunneled directly underneath that village, causing the sinkhole which destroyed several homes."

Scott shook his head. "No, that's just not true. I know all of the min-

THE SHEIK'S SIREN

ing companies that work in this region. The story about an illegal mine is just your enemy trying to create problems."

"And here," Zantar asked, pointing to the city on the map where Sheik Goran and Princess Calista had been kidnapped. "Do you know anything about why or how the leader of Silar and Princess Calista were kidnapped?" Zantar tilted his head as he watched the other man's face pale. "There are rumors that their kidnapping was an effort to distract the government from illegal mining activities. Your boss wouldn't be involved in these kinds of activities, right?"

Roland put a finger underneath the collar of his dress shirt, as if trying to loosen it. "I don't know anything about that."

The man lifted his hands in the air, palms out as if trying to ward off the danger he'd suddenly perceived. Apparently, Roland wasn't as much of an idiot as Zantar had thought. "Hey, I don't know what's going on there. I'm just here as a representative of my company, trying to get a road usage contract in place." He sidled over to the contract and flipped the pages. "We're even laying out repair costs, at our expense."

Zantar glanced down at the numbers, his eyes narrowing when he looked up at Roland. "Those aren't the same numbers that were emailed to my assistant last night." He waited, watching the man's mouth open slightly, but continued before the man spouted more lies. "In fact, those numbers are exactly twenty-five percent lower than what was in the contract sent to us last night." He shook his head. "That sounds like a bait and switch type of scam." He lowered his voice as he said, "You're not going to try and scam me, are you Mr. Roland?"

The idiot's nervous swallowing could probably be heard on the audio recording. "Never!"

Zantar ignored the lack of his title. The idiot man didn't know that he was supposed to use the title "Your Highness" or some other honorific when speaking to the ruler of Citran. It didn't really matter, Zantar supposed. The man was going to prison for a very long time.

"Good," Zantar replied, shifting his body slightly, then lifting his hand in the air. Roland didn't know that the hand signal was meant to hold off the law enforcement personnel who were stationed right outside the doorway. "First of all, I'd like you to take me to this brothel you mentioned."

Roland's pudgy features brightened and his whole demeanor changed to one of excitement. "Shouldn't we sign the contracts first?"

Zantar waved a hand towards the papers. "We'll get to that. I'm very intrigued by the stories you mentioned about these women."

Roland actually rubbed his hands together, delighted with the plan and visibly relieved that the previous illegal acts were no longer the topic of the conversation. "Let's go. I'll lead the way."

"No need for that. My team will drive us."

Twenty minutes later, they all arrived at the house in a relatively spread-out neighborhood. It looked more run-down than he'd anticipated, but Zantar didn't bother with that. He allowed his plain-clothed guards to accompany Roland into the house while the uniformed police stealthily moved around to surround the house. Moments later, after the police revealed themselves to the owners of the establishment, panic reigned. As expected, several idiots tried to escape and were quickly handcuffed and put into custody. The brothel owner, a woman in her mid-fifties who had probably been a victim of human trafficking herself by the looks of her rough appearance, was led out in handcuffs a few moments later. Roland was next and he was trying to pull away, yelling that he was a friend of "Zantar". That only caused his guards to handle him with less care.

His personal bodyguards drove Zantar back to the palace. "I want Roland questioned on the mining incidents. We'll need to inform Astir and Goran of this latest development. We also need to update Nasir. Some of the line items in that contract might impact his country as well. But even better, I think Roland might finally lead us to the head of this nest of vipers that have been plaguing those border villages before they can infiltrate Nasir's country."

Chapter 15

Five Months Later...

Faye stared at the plastic stick, not sure how she felt about the plus sign. Pregnant. She was pregnant with Zantar's child!

A flush of happiness almost overwhelmed her, and she sat back, staring at the computer. She'd bought the pregnancy test this morning, but it had taken her a few more hours to work up the courage to get an answer. During that time, she'd flipped between hope that she was pregnant to despair at not seeing Zantar, not sharing this news with him.

She was doing okay, she thought. She'd made it across the border into Citran and she was safe from Scott and his nasty threats. For now. Faye didn't fool herself into believing that he would disappear from her life. But for now, she needed to stop jumping at shadows and staring out the window at night, waiting for Scott, or some other boogey man, to break into her tiny apartment.

She had to keep reminding herself that she was more prepared now. She had more money saved up, and several new cell phones still in their packages that she just needed to activate if she felt as if she might be caught by Scott or someone who worked for him. She kept those "safe" and kept her bags packed at all times. Plus, she had a job. A job that paid better than housekeeping in a hotel. She'd finally found a job as a schoolteacher in a rural community. Teaching English was fun, she realized. In addition to her school position, she also tutored several students in art, showing them some skills to improve their painting efforts. She also offered babysitting services on the weekends.

Never again would she find herself in a vulnerable position! Scott had threatened her with lies and she hoped he burned in hell for what he'd done to her. But soon, very soon, she'd figure out a way to stop him from spreading those lies about her. In the meantime, she…her eyes dropped to the plastic strip. Smiling, she laid a hand over her stomach. A baby! She was going to have a baby! A little boy or girl that would look just like Zantar! Would they have a predisposition to his arrogant swagger? Faye certainly hoped so! Oh, how she would love to see that! She thought about Zantar and wondered what he was doing, wishing that she could talk to him, tell him about their child. She wanted so much for their child to grow up strong and healthy.

  She'd also figure out some way to let Zantar know about their child. She'd have to find him first. Glancing at the laptop, she relaxed her shoulders. She was very good at research. She'd eventually figure out where he lived.

  But right now, she had to finish her dissertation. She had to submit her research before her baby was born. That was the first step. The most important step!

  She'd figure out the rest later.

Chapter 16

Seven months later...

Faye glanced over at the clock, wondering how five minutes could last so long! Just five more minutes, and classes for the day would be over. She would rush over to Elspeth's house and pick up Shanta, her three-month-old baby daughter, and they could spend the weekend playing and having fun! Oh, how she missed her little baby during these long days at school! But her job gave her security and money. That money gave her the means to protect Shanta, allowed them to leave at a moment's notice if necessary.

Finally, the bell rang, and Faye waved goodbye to her students. "Have a good weekend!" she called out in English. Several of the students grinned back at her. "You too!" they responded, their English improving by leaps and bounds lately. She was so proud of them, but she still wanted them gone. She wanted to go find Shanta! Faye wanted to snuggle with her tiny daughter and find out what beautiful things she'd done over the day. More bubbles? How many times had Shanta wiggled her legs? Had she smiled? Oh, Faye prayed that Shanta didn't smile too often while Faye was working! No, that was crazy. Elspeth was a wonderful caregiver. Faye hoped that Shanta laughed and smiled and giggled all day while she was here at school.

Unfortunately, the fear of Scott finding them had never left Faye's mind. She constantly waited for Scott to find her and renew his threats, waiting for him to come around a corner, skulk out of a dark alley, or appear in either the doorway to her small classroom or the cottage where she and Shanta lived.

She still looked over her shoulder, still jumped at shadows, and still tensed every time the doorbell rang. Thankfully, her tension wasn't as bad as it had been when she'd first run away from his vile threats.

Faye wished that there was some way she could find out if Zantar was safe. Looking out the window of her classroom, she wondered if perhaps she could hire someone to find Zantar? Maybe...? Shaking her head, she focused on the students who were finishing up a quiz. Somehow, she'd find Zantar again. Once Scott couldn't threaten Zantar!

After leaving Skyla and finding a new place to hide, Faye had slowly started sleeping a bit better, but since Shanta's birth, that sleep had come in bits and spurts. Faye accepted that extreme, bone deep fatigue was just part of her life now.

The last bell rang and the students jumped up from their desks, grabbed their book bags and hurried out of the classroom, plopping their quiz down on her desk while calling out greetings in English to her. She smiled at each of them, proud of their progress.

But now, it was her turn to hurry out! Time to see Shanta!

Packing up her bag, Faye slung the strap over her shoulder and hurried out of the classroom, eager to leave the school and get to Shanta for their precious time together. A whole weekend! Maybe they'd go on a picnic? The weather was a bit cooler lately and...!

"Don't even try it!" the headmistress called out to Faye.

Faye turned, her fingers tightening on the strap of her bag as tension gripped her. Had Scott found her? Had he created pictures that made her look as if she'd been doing something bad? Or worse, had he found Zantar and...!

But the headmistress' features were smiling, almost excited! Faye didn't let her guard down. "What's up?" she asked as her boss approached.

"We have a special visitor today!" she replied, rushing down the hallway and straightening her clothing. "This is huge!"

"Huge?" Faye parroted. "In what way?"

"Sheik al Abouss is coming here for a visit!" she explained in an excited whisper, running a hand over her hair. "Apparently, there was some trouble in one of the villages last year. He is now traveling through the country, visiting even the small villages like ours to check on all of us. He wants to ensure that we are doing okay and that nothing is amiss."

"That's very..." she stopped, the name sounding familiar for some reason. "That's nice of him." She continued, her forehead wrinkling as she tried to place the name. Instantly, an image of Zantar popped into her mind. But that wasn't strange. He popped into her mind about a thousand times every day. She still loved him. She still cried for him at night. But at least she had Shanta to snuggle with during those long, lonely nights.

Zantar ground his teeth with frustration. These visits were necessary, but he was still furious that he hadn't found Faye. Several times, he'd told himself to give up. But those last words…I love you…kept haunting him. He loved her too, even though he was furious with her for running away.

His guards had haunted the small towns in Georgia where she had worked before starting her research, but none of her previous co-workers had heard from her. Damn her!

Yes, she'd warned him about Green Mining. After interrogating Scott Roland, the man had explained all of the mysterious events that had been happening in Skyla and Silar, as well as the constant caravans of trucks coming and going from the lone highway. Unfortunately, Roland didn't know who was in charge of Green Mining's parent company and hadn't offered any additional information on the illegal mining operations, other than what he'd developed on the border between Silar and Citran.

Would the man behind all of the illegal efforts ever be caught? Probably not. From what Roland had explained, no one really knew or saw the man. No one ever spoke to him. All instructions were done through second and third parties.

So why was Zantar traveling through all of these towns and villages? Why was he wasting his time?! He should focus on finding Faye!

Sighing, he tamped down on his frustration. This was his job, he reminded himself, forcing his shoulders to relax as he approached the headmistress of the village school. He refused to look to the right or left at the people gawking on the sidewalks. Faye wasn't in the crowds! She'd hidden herself away and…! And he wasn't here looking for Faye! He knew that she was long gone by now, hiding in fear of a non-existent threat.

If only she'd trusted him! If only she'd stuck around and told him whatever Roland had threatened her with! He could have told her that Roland was in a prison cell, rotting away. Furthermore, the guy wasn't faring well in prison. Word had gotten around to the other inmates about his actions, the way he'd hurt the women in the brothels and all of the women that had been kidnapped from small villages trafficked to the highest bidder. All of the inmates, men who knew that Roland had repeatedly raped the brothel's patrons, not to mention all of the environmental crimes! He was still waiting to be tried for those crimes. If there was ever a reason for Roland to be brought up for parole, Zantar would have those other charges brought forward and the man would be charged for those crimes as well.

No, the man was never getting out of prison.

Forcing his mind on the present, he moved forward, smiling politely at the group of teachers and staff members waiting on him in front of the school. "Good afternoon," he said to the woman who immediately bowed low.

"Your Highness!" the headmistress gushed, her face wreathed with smiles and excitement. "It's such an honor to have you here in our small town and, especially here at our school." She stepped back, waving her arm towards the other school employees. There were only about ten of them and Zantar allowed his eyes to briefly sweep over each of them. There was no time in the schedule to greet all of the teachers personally. He still had to meet with the town's governing body and visit the local health clinic before he could head back to the capital tonight.

He opened his mouth to utter the usual platitudes when his eyes stopped, arrested on a startled, beautiful face that had haunted his dreams every night for the past year!

"Faye!" he growled. It took him several moments, but when she blinked those long lashes, then stared right back at him with her beautiful, blue eyes, he spurred his muscles into movement, walking over to her. Without waiting for any response, he simply bent down and tossed her over his shoulder, carrying her to the SUV.

"No!" she screamed, instantly trying to get away from him. "Zantar, you can't do this! Please! I can't leave! I have to get to…" He shut the door on her outburst, tossing her into the back seat. Yes, he knew that it looked as if he'd just kidnapped one of the schoolteachers, but he didn't give a damn. He would find out what the hell she'd been up to for the last year and then he'd…hell, he had no idea what he'd do with her.

He heard her fist pounding on the window behind him, but he ignored her. Walking over to his guards, he whispered, "Get her to the helicopter and don't let her out of your sight!"

Then he walked over to the headmistress and took her hand. "I apologize," he told her with exaggerated politeness as he tried to calm the fury that was almost choking him.

For the past year, he'd been searching everywhere for Faye, and here she was, happy and thriving in a small town. HIS small town. He'd been driving his guards insane with his demands to find her, interrogating Roland over and over again, demanding to know different places Faye had vacationed, her school friends, her work friends. The stupid man didn't know much and was a pretty horrible brother, even for a step brother.

Zantar went through the motions with the teachers, but he didn't hear any of their comments when he spoke to the group, praising them for their skills, time, and compassion. All the while, his mind was on the woman who was currently going nuts inside the SUV. He wondered about that, but he was still too angry with her at the moment. She'd calm down, he told himself. And then they could have a rational conversation. Then he'd spank her pretty ass for putting him through the torment of the past year. Then he'd toss her pretty ass out of the country!

No, he wouldn't. Zantar came up with a variety of punishments for the beautiful woman. Up to and including keeping her locked up in his bedroom at the palace. Maybe even tied to the bed! Yes, that idea sounded pretty nice to him. He could then torture her with kisses every night, not satisfying her. Just as he'd endured over the past year! Every night, he'd dreamed about Faye. And every morning, he'd woken up feeling just as angry and furious and panicked when he realized she wasn't in his arms.

Now he would get his revenge. How dare she tell him she loved him, warn him about some criminal enterprise, then leave! Damn her!

His rage only increased as he moved back towards the SUV and she was staring out the window with tears streaming down her face.

He ignored the stab of pain that suddenly hit his chest. He wasn't going to give in to tears. Not after the past year. Not after…!

He opened the door, prepared to give her a tongue lashing. But as soon as the door was opened, she burst out, racing across the grassy field towards…he didn't know where she thought she was going because he grabbed her around the waist, hauling her back to the vehicle.

"No," he said with deadly calm, "you're not getting away from me this time," he explained smoothly.

"Shanta!" Faye said through stiff lips. "Shanta needs me. I should have picked her up from day care an hour ago! I need to get to her. Please, Zantar! I need to get to my baby!"

Baby?

The word exploded around him, his mind reeling. He might have even stumbled back slightly.

Baby!

"Please!" she gasped, her hands gripping his arm and her nails digging into the skin slightly as her urgency finally got through to him. "I need to get to her. She needs me!"

"Get in!" he ordered. "I'll drive you."

She got into the vehicle, but she wasn't very fast about it. Zantar was a bit more stunned, and he almost pushed her in to the interior. When she was seated, he pulled himself into the seat as well, slamming the door to the SUV with more force than was necessary. His guards moved quickly as well, everyone piling into the vehicles. He was so angry, he couldn't even speak. He couldn't ask questions. All he knew was that Faye had given birth to a…!

"Faye, is this…?" He couldn't even speak the words, the possibility too shocking.

She must have realized what his unspoken question was because she immediately nodded. "Yes. A few months after I escaped from Scott, I realized I was pregnant. Shanta is our daughter."

Two words hit him with that explanation. "Escape" and "Daughter" kept ringing in his ears. His guards must have understood as well because the guard in the front seat was immediately on his radio, issuing orders.

Zantar couldn't seem to speak. His mind wasn't able to process those two words, much less the ideas behind them. Daughter. Faye had a daughter. No…there was more to that. What had she said? "Our" daughter. Holy hell, Faye had given birth to his daughter?

The driver pulled up outside of a small house with a pretty garden. The sun was dipping down over the horizon at this point, so he knew that it was late. Later than usual, since an older woman in her fifties with streaks of grey in her dark hair, came out with a small bundle in her arms. The woman's smile disappeared as she watched the guards streak out of the SUVs, surrounding her house. The woman instantly clutched the small bundle to her breast, protecting the child.

Faye jumped out of the vehicle, rushing over to the woman. "It's okay, Elspeth," she said softly, reaching out for the small bundle. "It's okay!" she said again, her voice soothing.

Warily, the older woman transferred the small bundle into Faye's arms, still looking around with terror in her eyes.

Zantar took in all of this, still too stunned to speak or even process the information staring right back at him.

He stepped out of the vehicle and the elderly woman gasped, quickly dropping to her knees as Zantar approached. Zantar ignored the woman, his eyes focused on the small bundle in Faye's arms. Faye looked down at the older woman, obviously confused. "Elspeth?" she called out, shifting the bundle to the side as she peered down at the woman.

"Your Highness!" Elspeth whispered, awe in her voice but she kept her head bowed, her hands on the ground.

Zantar looked down at the woman briefly, then said, "Please stand."

Faye was very confused, but at least she was holding Shanta in her arms. Her little daughter was safe. Instantly, Elspeth lurched to her feet, but kept her head bowed, her whole body subservient. It was so unlike the kind woman, Faye wasn't sure what was going on.

She turned and looked up at Zantar. "Who are you?" she asked.

Elspeth gasped, stepping back as she swiveled her head from Faye to Zantar. "You don't know?" she asked in horror.

"Know what?"

Zantar lifted his hand, stopping the other woman's explanation. "Please," he choked out, staring down at the baby in Faye's arms. "Is this...?"

"Yes," Faye replied, smiling up at Zantar shyly now. "This is our daughter, Zantar. I named her Shanta." She laughed softly, then continued, "I would have named her Zanta or some other feminine form of your name, but as soon as the nurse put her into my arms after the delivery, the name Shanta seemed to fit."

Zantar stared at the bundle with dark hair and dark eyes. Her skin was pale, just like Faye's, but the rest of the infant looked just like him. Or was he only seeing what he wanted to see? Apparently, even Elspeth saw the similarities because she gasped again, her eyes still moving from the infant to his face.

Faye moved closer. "I'm sorry I was so frantic back at the school. It's just that...well, I don't like being away from Shanta. Earlier, I was terrified that you'd take me away and I wouldn't see her. I was supposed to pick her up right after classes finish." She shrugged slightly and moved one of her hands, allowing the small girl to wrap her tiny fingers around one of Faye's fingers.

"You were pregnant when you disappeared?"

Faye sighed, nodding. "I didn't know it at the time. I was so focused on getting away from Scott and making sure that you didn't sign any contract with him. And then I was too busy traveling and researching that company, Green Mining, afraid that they would do something horrible to another town. I started writing letters to any government agency that I could, warning them of their illegal activities. So by the time I realized I was pregnant, I was already five months along."

Zantar looked around, noticing that his guards were looking around nervously. "We need to leave," he stated firmly, taking her arm and guiding her back to the SUV. "We're too exposed."

"Exposed?" Faye asked, skipping along next to him. "I don't understand."

"Come," he told her, urging her faster. He kept glancing down at Shanta and Faye wanted to stop him, demand answers. But he was acting so strangely, she didn't understand so she simply moved along with him.

Zantar couldn't believe it. A daughter! He was a father? A father! The infant looked up at him, obviously sensing that something strange was happening to her world. He shook his head, still trying to grasp the full meaning of his current situation. He had a daughter!

"We can't get into the SUV!" she whispered, pulling Shanta closer to her chest. "It's not safe!"

Zantar stared at Faye, not understanding. Or more to the point, Faye didn't understand. He suddenly realized that Faye had no idea who he was! She knew that he was wealthy, but Faye had no concept of who he was or the enormity of his power and wealth.

"Get in the vehicle, Faye. You're not safe out here. Nor is Shanta." Damn, he liked that name! It was sweet and feminine. Princess Shanta. It had a nice ring to it! Shanta al Abbous. Princess Shanta al Abbous!

Astir and Goran both had children now. What would happen if he betrothed Shanta to…what the hell was he thinking?! He hadn't even held his daughter in his arms and already he was betrothing her to a kid she didn't know?

He was insane. That was the only explanation. He rubbed his forehead as Faye and Shanta stepped into the SUV. He strapped her into the seat while Faye held Shanta securely in her arms. The driver pulled away, driving carefully through the streets of the small village. Everyone was silent, exploring their own thoughts. Zantar kept looking down at Shanta. And every time he looked at her, she was staring right back up at him. Their eyes looked exactly the same. But on her, they were prettier. Darker. She had long, dark lashes surrounding those dark eyes and she looked…beautiful! His beautiful daughter.

The helicopter was ready for takeoff, and Zantar realized that the whipping of the helicopter blades was terrifying Shanta. Well, it was scaring Faye as well.

"Let me hold her. My upper body is bigger. I can shield her more from the sounds of the helicopter and the winds." Zantar asked.

Faye glanced around, assessing the situation, then nodded. "She's nervous. Shanta doesn't understand what's going on." But she shifted the child into his arms, reluctantly.

Zantar swallowed, nervous now. His daughter! Damn, he had a daughter!

The vehicle stopped, his guards rushing to form a perimeter. Faye and Zantar both ducked against the wind as they stepped out of the SUV, Zantar using his entire body to shield both Shanta and Faye against the whipping of the wind caused by the helicopter blades getting ready for takeoff. But Shanta cried regardless of his efforts.

He stepped into the helicopter, all three of them surrounded by his

THE SHEIK'S SIREN

guards, then the helicopter took off. They flew through the night air, all other air traffic diverted for the time while he was in the air. Until they landed on the roof of the palace, no other flights would be allowed nearby other than the military planes that were always flying around his air space, protecting him, and now his family.

Damn, he had a family!

The helicopter landed on the helipad located on the roof of the palace. Normally, Zantar would simply step out of the helicopter, unconcerned about the whipping winds caused by the helicopter blades. But this time…looking down, he noticed that Shanta's pretty brown eyes were glancing around, her hands fisting on her chest as she tried to understand this new world.

"Turn off the engine," he called out to the helicopter pilot, thinking of how scared Shanta had been when they'd boarded the flight.

The pilot looked at him with surprise, but then his eyes glanced down at the infant who looked ready to scream with terror, her tiny, lower lip trembling. Immediately, the pilot flipped several switches. The sound immediately faded, but it took several more moments before the blades slowed enough for them to exit.

Still, Zantar curved his body around the infant, his daughter, shielding her as best he could. He wanted to protect her from the world! He finally understood why Faye had become so crazed when she'd thought that her daughter was in danger. It was an overwhelming emotion.

They entered the palace and Faye clung to him, her blue eyes just as huge as Shanta's while the three of them made their way to his suite.

Once they were finally alone, he turned and handed Shanta back to Faye. "What does she eat?"

He noticed Faye's cheeks turn pink and he was even more curious. "She…um…I need a place to nurse her."

"You're…" he couldn't say the words, but his eyes moved to her breasts. The same breasts that had so fascinated him a year ago, they were now providing sustenance to his daughter!

"You can…" he cleared his throat and pointed towards the sofa. "Is that okay?"

She looked over at the sofa, then nodded. "I just need privacy."

He shook his head, his arrogance back in place once more. "There's no chance that I'm letting you out of my sight."

Faye's shoulders tightened and she looked up at him. "Do you think I'll try and sneak away? I didn't run away from–"

"No," he replied quickly, interrupting her explanation. But the reality was that, yes, he was thinking that she might slip away from him again. "I just…" he sighed, rubbing a hand along the back of his neck. "Faye,

I'm a bit lost here. I...I don't want to..." he stopped trying to understand exactly what he was failing to explain. "I don't want to miss anything else." Yes, that was it. He felt as if he'd lost something and suddenly found it. Now he didn't want to lose Faye, or Shanta, again!

Faye stared up at him, finally understanding. "I get that." She tilted her head towards the sofa, looking awkward and unsure of herself. "Okay...well..." she sighed and tried to assess the area, although he wasn't sure what might be missing. Finally, she explained, "I need pillows."

"Pillows?" he repeated. "Why?"

Faye smiled slightly, her cheeks turning pink. "Because even though she's only three months old, she gets a bit heavy for me when I'm nursing her."

"I can hold her," he asserted firmly, even moving forward to take Shanta out of her arms. Faye laughed nervously, turning her body so that he couldn't take Shanta away. "That's not going to help me feed her."

He sighed, his eyes looking at the small child with longing.

Faye understood the need in his eyes and reacted to it, offering, "How about if I feed her, then you can read her stories and rock her to sleep?" Faye looked around. "Where will she sleep tonight? I have a bassinet at my place. We could...?"

"My staff is getting supplies," he explained. "A crib, bassinet, stroller... anything you need, you just have to ask, and it will be brought here to you."

"Ah!"

She bit her lower lip and looked around. "Well, I guess I should..." Faye stopped speaking when Shanta squawked in protest, her mouth reaching for and not finding Faye's breast.

"I have to hurry," Faye announced. "Shanta is hungry and she doesn't..."

Faye's words were drowned out by Shanta's furious cry. Faye walked over to the sofa, unbuttoning her blouse with one hand and settling down in the corner.

She was self-conscious as she settled both of them on the sofa, releasing her breast from the ugly nursing bra so that Shanta could attach. By the time Faye had pulled several pillows over to prop up her daughter's little body, Shanta was feeding hungrily, both of her tiny hands fisted on Faye's breast as she nursed.

"She's beautiful," Zantar said, his voice husky as he watched.

"Please sit down," Faye asked. "You're too tall for me to see you when you're standing like that."

Zantar sat, but his eyes continued to watch.

There was a long silence and Shanta finished on one side. Faye turned her daughter around, feeling the heat in her cheeks when she had to expose her other breast. But Zantar seemed oblivious of her embarrassment and continued to watch, fascinated by the process.

"Does it hurt?" he asked.

Faye shrugged, trying to ignore the heat staining her cheeks. "It hurt like the devil initially. But we've figured things out," she said, running a finger over Shanta's soft fuzzy head. The dark tufts were sticking straight up on top of her daughter's head, but the back of her head was bald where the bassinet's mattress had worn away her precious hair.

"She's beautiful," he commented.

"I agree," Faye said, brushing that fingertip over Shanta's cheek. Finally, Faye looked up. "You didn't sign the contracts with Green Mining, did you?"

Zantar pulled his eyes away from Faye. "No. After you..." he sighed, still trying to ease the anger at her departure. He rubbed the back of his neck and started over. "After your abrupt departure, I looked into the company a bit more. Turns out, Green Mining isn't really a company at all. It's only a shell corporation used for tax evasion and criminal activities."

"So...?"

"Scott Roland, your step brother, was convicted of rape, human trafficking, kidnapping, abuse of humanity, tax evasion, burglary, assault, sexual assault, attempted robbery, and is awaiting trial on a slew of other crimes." He leaned back in his chair. "He was the representative for Green Mining which had been digging tunnels underneath villages in order to mine efiasia, which is a mineral that can be used to build cheap microchips. Gold is the best mineral because it doesn't rust and has fast conductive qualities. Efiasia is a newly discovered mineral that several of the lower quality computer manufacturers are using to build cheap laptops. The microchips in these computers aren't nearly as good for long term use, but the mineral will last for about a year or two before breaking down, which renders the computer useless."

"Why was Scott in Skyla?"

"Actually, he kept driving back and forth from the capital city in Skyla, to Citran where he was in charge of the mining activities here." At her surprise, he nodded and continued. "There's a massive efiasia deposit that straddles four countries. The first company that was created to cover the mining activities simply dug underneath one of the villages in Skyla. But that created a massive area of instability that caused a small village to fall into the mine. Initially, it looked like a sink hole."

Faye's eyes widened. "And then?"

"The mining company learned its lessons there, but the deposit was large enough that they could come at it from a different angle. The next time, they started operations far enough outside of a small town, and they kidnapped Sheik Goran el Istara of Skyla and his fiancée, now his wife, Princess Calista del Taran, in order to distract the government so that the mining company could do whatever it wanted."

"That's horrible! What happened to the Sheik and his…wife? And what about the first village?"

"Thankfully, no one was hurt, but almost every building in the town was damaged. The town is being rebuilt and the residents are stronger than ever."

Faye looked down at Shanta, shuddering with the horror of what was going on. "That's something, at least."

"Sheik Goran and Princess Calista are married now. No harm done to them."

Faye smiled, nodding as she looked down again. Shanta was slowing down, exhausted from the shock of her day as well as a full belly.

"The mining company didn't stop there, although they moved their operations out of Silar and Skyla. But because of the large deposit of the mineral and the potential profits, the company merely moved their operations. "Thankfully, we were able to figure out what they were trying to do this time and stop them before life or property were damaged."

"Oh my gosh!"

"Exactly," Zantar replied, sighing with frustration over the entire situation. "It wasn't until the leaders of Skyla and Silar brought me and Sheik Nasir, the leader of Minar, together that we figured out that all of the issues were related." He shook his head. "But it wasn't until you told me not to sign contracts with Green Mining that we were able to put everything together."

"So…?"

Zantar took her free hand, holding it in his larger one. "It's done, Faye," he assured her. "We stopped them. With your help. It took several months to get all of the truck drivers and excavators rounded up, but because you told us about Green Mining, we had the clue that we needed."

She smiled, snapping her nursing bra closed with one hand, then buttoning her shirt. When she was once again covered, she looked up at Zantar, gently patting Shanta's diaper-clad bottom. "That's good. And everyone is okay?"

"So far, we haven't found any true victims, except for the mountain areas. They were severely damaged by the tunnels. But otherwise, we stopped them before anyone was hurt."

She smiled, glancing down shyly with his praise. "That's good."

Zantar leaned forward, bracing his elbows on his knees as he looked intently at her. "If you'd believed in me, you could have been part of the solution, Faye," he told her.

Faye stared at him, stunned by his assertion. "What do you mean?"

Zantar watched her carefully, feeling his anger increase. "You kissed me, Faye. You made love with me, told me that you loved me, and then walked out of my life." His eyes dropped to his daughter. "And then you took away my opportunity to experience our daughter's birth and the first months of life from me." He heard her gasp, but couldn't pull back the words. He couldn't soften them. "You didn't trust me to help you!"

Faye's lips opened slightly and he saw a touch of tears in her eyes. "I couldn't! You don't know how bad Scott is!" she asserted, starting to sit up but the movement jerked Shanta out of her happy place, so Faye forced herself to relax once again. She lifted her chin, glaring at him. "Scott was using me to get to you. He was going to force me to manipulate you and I wouldn't allow that."

Zantar stood up, trying to come to terms with everything. A lot was happening and he wasn't sure what he was feeling. "How about if you tell me what the hell happened? You owe me an explanation."

Faye stared down at their daughter for a long moment and Zantar wasn't sure what she was thinking. Thankfully, a moment later, she lifted her eyes, which were now filled with tears, and started to talk. "That day," she said, choking on the word, "that last day, Scott accosted me on the street. He looked horrible." She shook her head. "Well, I guess it was actually the day before. He approached me and demanded money from me. But I didn't have very much."

"I already know about that." He rubbed a hand over his face. "What happened the next day?"

She sighed. "Scott approached me again. He was even nastier this time."

Zantar's eyes narrowed on her and he suddenly remembered something she'd said earlier today. Amid all of the revelations, it was taking him a bit of time to process each of them. But he was starting to understand. "How did he threaten you?"

Faye's eyes blinked and his body tightened with anger. This time, it wasn't directed at her. It was firmly directed towards the man currently sitting in a prison cell.

"He told me that, if I didn't somehow convince you to sign the contracts with the mining company, then he would create videos or pictures of me with some of my students." She lowered her head. "Actually, I can't remember if the images would be of me and my students or just teenage boys." She shuddered. "It doesn't matter. As a high school teacher, that threat was an evil one." Faye brushed a hand over Shanta's cheek again. "He said he'd make the pictures as disgusting as possible." She looked up at him, her eyes filled with tears now. "I've never hurt a child, Zantar! Never! And the idea of any teacher, male or female, taking advantage of a student is repugnant!"

"I agree," he replied, then came over to her. "I'm sorry that you endured his threats. But you…" he stopped, shaking his head. "You should have come to me and told me what he'd said."

She nodded, angrily wiping away the tears. "Yes, I should have. But then he threatened you!" She nodded when his face froze. "He said he'd kill you if I didn't get you to sign the papers." She closed her eyes, pressing her lips together in remembered panic. "And if that threat hadn't worked, he would have come up with another. And another! He wanted to get to you through me. I figured…." She stopped, a sob ripping through her at the terrifying memories. "I figured that, if I wasn't around you anymore, then he couldn't hurt you. You would be safe." She shook her head, then glanced down at Shanta once more. "If I'd known how to get in touch with you, I would have told you about Shanta as soon as I'd figured out that I was pregnant. For a long time, I just thought I was sick because of the stress of trying to stay ahead of Scott. He sent out people to find me and several times he got pretty close."

"No, Faye," he explained gently. "The people you ran from were my guards. It was my team trying to find you!" His anger towards her was softening now that she'd explained Roland's threats.

She stared at him, stunned by this latest revelation. At that point, all she could say was, "Oh!"

His hand ruffed up his hair as he started pacing. "I'm not sure if I'm angry with you or with myself."

Faye felt the same way. She suspected that she should be angry at him, but she wasn't sure why. She'd run away from him to save him, and herself, from Scott's viciousness. So…why would she be angry towards him? Or was she angry with herself for believing in Scott's threats?

Focusing on Zantar for the moment, because her own feelings were a bit too confusing, she asked, "Why would you be angry with yourself?"

He stopped pacing and shook his head, his hands fisted on his hips as he chuckled at the past year. "Because I never told you who I was," he explained, turning to face her. "I was being selfish."

Faye blinked, startled by his declaration. "Selfish? How were you being selfish?"

He sighed, shaking his head slightly. "You were the first woman who wanted me for who I am, not because of my title, Faye."

She stared at him, biting her lip. A moment later, she looked around at the luxury, then shrugged as she brought her eyes back up to his harsh features. "I'm still not completely sure what your title is, Zantar."

He laughed and sat back down in the chair. Faye felt Shanta fall asleep and adjusted her daughter in her arms, letting the pillows take more of her weight.

"I'm Zantar al Abbous, Sheik of Citran. I'm ruler of this country. I was in Skyla that week we were together trying to figure out what the hell was going on with the border villages." He laughed harshly. "It was all connected. The sink holes, the trucks disturbing the villages at night, the tunnels going from the caves in the mountains to the drilling sites, the Green Mining operations and the kidnappings…everything was connected. We know that now. Scott Roland was behind the tunnels and he's in prison now."

"And you stopped him!" She paused, closing her eyes for a long moment so she could savor that news once more.

He smiled grimly, nodding his head. "Yes, you're safe, Faye. You and Shanta are safe from Roland's threats." That's when his eyebrows pulled down as he looked back at her. "And that's why you should have trusted me instead of simply kissing me and disappearing."

She nodded, looking directly into his eyes. "I know." Faye's lips pressed together and she nodded again for emphasis. "I'm sorry. That was wrong of me."

Zantar was stunned. An apology? She was…sorry? Everything inside of him relaxed and he wasn't sure where to go with that. He hadn't expected her to apologize, but her simple words melted all of the anger and fear that had plagued him for the past year. Was it really that simple?

Staring into her blue eyes, he knew that it was.

"Did you mean it?"

She blinked, confused now. "Mean what?"

"What you said that day?"

Her lips lifted slightly and Faye nodded, easing the rest of the pain. "Yes. I meant it." She blinked slightly. "I love you, Zantar. And I've missed you every moment of the past year!"

He moved over to her, bracing a hand on either side of her shoulders against the back of the sofa. "Don't say that unless you intend to follow through on what that means, Faye!"

"I mean it!" she replied with heat. "I don't know what you mean about following through but..." she stopped and lifted her hand, touching his cheek. "But I love you! And I've missed you so much!"

He looked down at the now sleeping infant. "Can you put her into the crib?"

"Crib?" Faye chirped, still focused on his handsome features. "Has a crib already been delivered for her? I know that you said someone would...well..." she sighed, her shoulders drooping slightly. "Zantar, this is all very new to me. I don't understand..."

"What's wrong, Faye?" he asked, his rough fingers touching her cheek.

Faye looked down at Shanta. "I was just going to...I don't know. Create a makeshift place for her to sleep. Maybe surround her with pillows or something."

He rolled his eyes and pushed up. "I told you that my staff was providing everything."

"I know you did." She pulled her eyes away from Shanta's sleeping features and looked into his eyes. "Zantar, I'm not used to having servants. This is all new to me." She sighed again. "As is trusting someone to do things for me. Like fight for me."

He froze and stared into her blue eyes. "Is that why you ran away?"

"Yes. I think so. I'm used to dealing with all of my problems. Zantar. I'm used to being on my own, fighting my own battles. I've been on my own, essentially ever since the moment my mother married my stepfather. It was just...easier to stay out of their way. To avoid Scott when he came home for his college breaks and...well, I learned to only rely on myself."

"So you ran."

"Yes," she replied with a nod. "It wasn't a lack of trust in you," she finally explained. "It was a knee-jerk reaction. Running was the only solution I could come up with. If Scott couldn't find me, then he couldn't use me to get to you. Problem solved." She shrugged, still patting Shanta's bottom. "It's my way."

"I'm going to have to teach you other ways," Zantar explained. Then he took her hand and tugged her up from the sofa. "Come with me." He then led her into a small room where a crib, changing table and even a rocking chair had been set up.

Faye halted in the doorway, stunned by the lovely furniture as well as stacks of diapers. "How in the world did this happen?" she asked with awe. "Did you borrow all of this from someone? Or was it already here?"

"Everything is new, specifically purchased for Shanta," he countered.

"If you don't like the style then I can-"

"I love it," Faye interrupted, still stunned by the efficiency of whoever had accomplished all of this in such a short period of time. "It's perfect!"

She walked over to the changing table and set Shanta carefully down on the cushioned area. "Would you like to change her?"

Zantar stared down at the tiny human being, then shook his head. As much as he wanted to touch her, hold her and get to know his tiny daughter, he was terrified of her fragility as well. "No. I'll just watch this first time."

Faye laughed, then efficiently grabbed a diaper off of the top of the stack, as well as a fleece pajama outfit. It took Faye very little time to change her daughter's diaper and put her into the one piece outfit, made easier because Shanta was blissfully sleeping. Thankfully, the tiny girl would continue to sleep for at least another four hours, she thought.

When Shanta was completely changed, Faye lifted her up and bounced Shanta as she walked over to the beautiful crib, placing her in the center. She then stepped back, giving Zantar more room. "You can touch her if you'd like. She won't break."

Zantar looked at Faye sharply, then glanced back down at the little girl. "She's too small," he growled.

Faye laughed. "I thought so too when she was first born. But she's a tough little lady."

Zantar reached out and, carefully touched Shanta's fluffy hair, smoothing it down slightly. "She's beautiful."

Faye smiled at the repeated comment, touching Shanta's fleece covered foot. "I think so."

Zantar turned to look at her, his eyes heating up. "You are as well, Faye."

She looked at him, her eyes wide. "I thought you were angry with me."

He sighed and pulled her into his arms. "I am." He then shook his head. "No. I understand now. You were trying to protect me. And yourself." His arms tightened and he groaned. "Yes. I am still angry. But I'm not sure why."

Faye snuggled against his chest. "I understand."

As he held her in his arms, his anger eased even more. Faye was here. She was safe and...his eyes kept straying to the small crib. He couldn't see Shanta from this angle, but just knowing she was here...hell, he was still stunned. A daughter! He had a daughter!

His arms tightened around Faye. Five hours ago, he hadn't known what he was going to do if he'd ever found Faye again. Now his path was clear.

Chapter 17

"Married?" Faye gasped, bouncing Shanta in her arms the following morning.

"Yes," Zantar replied. "Married."

Faye shook her head, trying to figure out what was going on. She was tired, having gotten only about four hours of sleep last night. Plus, those four hours had been broken up. She'd jerked awake only to find herself safe with Zantar's arms still around her. They'd both been fully dressed, which had only confused her further.

Now he was standing in front of her, announcing that they needed to get married. Her world...last night she'd been confused. Now she felt as if quicksand was swallowing her up!

"But Zantar, we can't..."

"We must!" he reiterated firmly. "For Shanta's benefit, we must be married."

Oh, that hurt! Faye turned away, trying to hide the pain lashing at her from his words.

If only he'd said that they needed to be married because he couldn't live without her, that he'd been searching for her while she'd been in hiding. That he loved her and had missed her!

She sighed, squeezing her eyes closed as tears threatened once again. If she'd learned anything over the past year, it was that life wasn't a fairy tale. It was harsh and brutal and generally completely unfair.

"Fine," she whispered, giving in to his demand. In that instant, she also gave up her hopes of love and a man who wanted her so badly, he'd get down on his knees and tell her of his undying love.

"The ceremony will take place this afternoon."

Faye's eyes opened with a jerk, and she spun back around to stare at him. "This afternoon?" She looked down at Shanta, who was still crying, still uncomfortable for some reason. She had a dry diaper and a full belly. But Shanta squawked and cried out, refusing to be comforted.

"Yes. We will have a small wedding, just a few important guests."

Faye sighed, trying to force her mind to work through the confusion caused by…well, by the chaos of the past twenty-four hours, lack of sleep and…yeah, the lack of sleep was the biggest issue.

"Fine," she whispered, wanting to curl up into a ball. She was just tired, she thought. And frustrated. And she didn't know what was wrong with Shanta!

"Is something wrong with our daughter?" he demanded, his eyes sharpening on the tiny bundle that was his daughter. Faye smiled tearily at the use of "our". At least he wasn't doubting Shanta's paternity, she thought. That was something, wasn't it?

"She's just cranky," Faye explained but her frazzled, frantic feelings only increased as Shanta wiggled and groused about…something.

"Is it because you are so tired?"

Faye laughed heartily at that question. "Zantar, I've been tired for the past twelve-plus months." She gestured to the dark circles under her eyes. "This isn't anything different from any other day."

His lips compressed and, instantly, Faye felt guilty for telling him that.

"Why don't you give Shanta to the nanny that I hired? Give yourself a small break. Maybe take a short nap?"

Faye shook her head, dismissing his suggestion. "I'm not giving Shanta to a stranger, just because…"

"Faye," he interrupted, smiling slightly with a gentle shake of his head. "You're going to become my wife. You will be surrounded by servants that are here to help you with whatever you need."

Faye didn't know how to respond to that, so she simply pressed her lips together and bounced Shanta faster. Her arms ached and there were shoots of pain spiking up her back, but she still didn't feel comfortable handing her cranky daughter off to a stranger just because Shanta wasn't being sweet and wonderful.

"I'm fine," she told him.

"You're not fine, Faye!" he snapped. "You weren't fine a year ago and you wouldn't let me help you!" He threw his hands in the air, his frustration intensifying. "How can I get you to trust me? And if not trust, then how about just letting me help you?"

Faye was startled, but her nerves were right on the edge. Shanta also chose that moment to go from cranky to outright furious and announced her state of mind with a loud wail.

"Fine!" she snapped right back at him and walked over to Zantar. "You want to help? You soothe her!" she said and transferred their cranky daughter into Zantar's arms, then walked out of the room.

Zantar stared down at his daughter, who had abruptly gone silent, and suspected that he had the same stunned look on his face. Father and daughter stared into each other's similar eyes, both trying to figure out if they liked this new situation.

For his part, Zantar shifted his daughter in his arms, wondering if her tiny fists and bouncing arms was a problem. Should she be this small? Was this normal? And was she about to wail again?

"Hello," he said awkwardly, then cleared his throat. He felt ridiculous, but also wanted to introduce himself to the infant daughter. "I'm your father," he told her, reverting to a stern voice. "And we are going to get along famously." She didn't look impressed. Her eyes remained unconvinced while her mouth opened, her red lips looking as if she wanted to say something, but like him, she wasn't sure what words would suffice at the moment.

"You're not going to be betrothed as my mother was," he vowed. "You will choose your own husband." He pulled her even closer, shifting her so that he could see her more clearly. "And you will be happy. I guarantee that."

He took a tentative step and, when Shanta didn't scream in protest, he took another. And another. They walked around the room and Zantar explained his world, telling her about all of the things he would teach her. "You will be an expert with horses. We will ride along the dunes. Your first horse will be a pony though," he told her with an admonishing voice. "You must learn slowly. And you will also care for your own horse. There is a bond that forms when you brush down your horse. You connect with the animal and she or he connects with you. It helps both of you to understand each other. That will make you a better rider."

Zantar nodded firmly with that. "And you will be good with our people. I will introduce you to the world and they will adore you. Just as I do," he continued with a gruff voice, unaware of how his arms were now bouncing the small girl in his arms.

Faye stood outside of the room, looking around and wondering where she would go. She'd stormed out of the bedroom in a huff, furious with Zantar for his announcement that they would marry this afternoon as well as his admonition that she should give their daughter over to someone else and…well, everything! She was just so confused! And overwhelmed.

She'd tried to be calm yesterday when she'd first seen Zantar in the school yard, as well as afterwards when he'd shuffled her and Shanta into the SUV and then the helicopter and then into this magnificent palace where she didn't know anyone and didn't understand what was going on!

Faye was scared. That was the real problem, she told herself. She was terrified! This was a strange world! What was she supposed to do? How should she act? She'd loved Zantar a year ago, but that was before she had known who he really was! The man was a freaking world leader? How had she missed that? How had she not known that the man ruled an entire country?

Rubbing her forehead, she paced along the expanse of the beautifully decorated room. It was filled with large sofas, an immense television and strange electronic components that were probably a state of the art sound system. But Faye couldn't figure out how to turn on the television. Besides, she'd done without television ever since arriving in Skyla to do her research and…! Her computer! All of her work was on that computer! Her research, her dissertation! Her lesson plans and her whole life! She accessed her bank, paid her bills, and connected to her friends from that computer! It had all of her contacts on it and the device was back at the school, locked away in her classroom locker!

Turning, she headed right back to Zantar, ready to demand that he find her laptop and bring it to her. But Faye stopped in the doorway, listening to Zantar talk about horses and diplomacy. He also vowed that she wouldn't be betrothed to anyone for political reasons and…was that still a thing?!

Her heart melted. The surge of love she felt for this man was overwhelming, bringing back all of the memories that she'd savored over the past year without him. He was…magnificent. Shanta wasn't crying. She wasn't even cranky. She was fascinated as she got used to the newest person in her life. Her father. Wow! Shanta now had a daddy!

And Faye still loved him! With all of her heart, she loved this man!

"Yes!" she whispered. Faye hadn't meant to speak the word out loud. Nor had she meant for Zantar to hear her. But as soon as she spoke the word, he spun around, his eyebrows lifted in inquiry.

"Yes?"

Faye watched as he wiggled his finger with Shanta's tiny fist holding it. Nodding, she said even louder, "Yes!" Faye walked into the room, feeling confident if a bit terrified of the future. With this man? Yes. Only with Zantar.

"Yes…what?" he asked, needing clarification.

"I just remembered why I fell in love with you," she whispered, then lifted up onto her toes to kiss him. It was just a brief brush of her lips

THE SHEIK'S SIREN

against his, then she pulled away, but Faye could see the heat in his eyes. Confusion too!

"Yes, you'll marry me this afternoon?"

Faye laughed. "A half hour ago, you acted as if I didn't have a choice."

He sighed, his shoulders tight. "You have a choice, Faye."

"I choose you," she whispered.

Faye heard the growl in his voice and laughed. "I want to hold you," he announced. "But I'm also pretty amazed with my daughter. I don't think I'm willing to give her up just yet."

Faye smiled, her heart aching with love for Zantar. "She's pretty cute, isn't she?" She looked down at Shanta's adorable expression, smiling at her and Faye tickled her tummy.

"Both of you are beautiful."

Faye looked up at him now. "I still love you, Zantar. That never died."

He groaned, then bent again to kiss her. This time, it was a bit longer.

"I'm going to introduce you to the nanny," he warned her. "We need to talk."

She nodded, then pulled back. "Okay. Let's talk."

Zantar called out and, instantly, an older, very confident-looking woman stepped into the room. Zantar handed Shanta off to the woman who smiled and cooed, obviously very proficient at holding infants. "Faye, this is Medira. She has cared for the children of four other royal families. She understands the protocols and has a master's degree in early childhood development."

Faye watched as the older woman cradled Shanta in her arms, smiling down at the girl. Shanta wasn't sure about this newest person, but she didn't scream out in protest. Faye wanted to argue that it was too many new things for the infant. But the woman didn't take Shanta away. In fact, she simply walked over to one of the chairs and sat down, whispering "secrets" to the little girl.

Medira looked up at Faye and smiled. "I would be honored to care for your daughter for however long you need. If you'd like just a thirty-minute break, I can stay right here. We'll just get to know each other while you are within hearing distance. But you can rush over if Shanta needs you, if that is okay with you?"

The woman spoke with a British accent, but Faye suspected that the woman spoke several languages since she'd spoken to Shanta in Arabic.

Plus, her suggestion eased the nervousness inside of Faye.

"Thank you!" she said, relieved that Shanta wouldn't be carried away to some mysterious and far-away nursery.

"This way," Zantar said, taking Faye's hands to lead her into another room, this one fitted out with only four chairs around a low, polished table. The walls were filled with shelves of books and there was a bar in one corner. This was a man's library, she thought with amusement as she sat down in one of the chairs.

But before she could relax, Zantar took her hands and pulled her up, right into his arms. He kissed her then, a soul-searching, mind-drenching, passion-inducing kiss that made her toes curl with desire.

"Will you say it again?" he asked.

Faye was startled by his question. He waited, wondering if she'd admit it. He could see the answer in her eyes though.

"Yes," she finally replied. "I still love you." She sighed, leaning her head against his chest. "I never stopped loving you."

He lowered his head, one hand lifting her head so that he could kiss her lightly but his other arm tightened around her waist. "Don't ever leave me, Faye!" he growled.

"Why? Because…?"

"Because…" he paused, sighing and laying his forehead against hers. "Because I missed you too much." He growled. "Because you make my world…brighter."

Faye smiled, enchanted by this gruff, powerful man as he avoided telling her that he loved her. She wasn't letting him off the hook though. She needed to hear the words. After the last year, she needed the assurance that his feelings for her were stronger than mere caring. "So…that means that you…?"

She paused, waiting for him to fill in the blanks.

"I feel…very…strongly for you, Faye."

She laughed, shaking her head. "Zantar, I need…"

"I love you, damn it!" he snarled, picking her up into his arms and squeezing her. "I love you to distraction. There! Is that what you wanted to hear? That I can't stand the thought of you not being here! That the idea of you being in another man's arms makes me want to smash the man's face. And abuse my position by tossing him into prison and forgetting about him!" He lifted her up into his arms, carrying her out of the library. "Is that what you needed to hear?"

"Yes!" she replied, laughing and wrapping her arms around his neck as she hugged him. "Yes, that's exactly what I needed to hear!"

There was a growl in his voice as he carried her back through the room they had just left. Medira looked up and smiled reassuringly. Shanta was holding a colorful toy, oblivious to her parents' absence at the moment.

"She's fine," Zantar assured Faye as he carried her down a short hallway and…into the bedroom!"

"You're going to make me crazy, woman!" he warned her as he laid her down on the bed, then moved over her, covering her with his body. "I love you!" he said, this time the words were simple and powerful and he followed that statement with a kiss against her lips.

"That works too," she whispered, her love for this man overwhelming her.

"Any chance you might want more kids?" he asked, shifting so that their bodies were more perfectly aligned.

Faye groaned, arching against him now. "I don't think that's a fair question to ask me when I've only had three or four hours of sleep."

He bent to nibble at the base of her throat, creating another kind of moan from her. "So if I were to ask in…say…another couple of months, you might have a different answer?"

She laughed this time. "It's possible. But I'm not going to promise anything until I get more sleep!"

"Fair enough," he said, then proceeded to strip off her clothes and discover all of the lovely ways that pregnancy hand changed her body. His fingers and mouth, tongue and even his teeth explored, teased and tasted every part of her body. He paused at the silver lines along her hips, kissing them and stroking her inner thighs when she started to become self-conscious. He moved lower and lower, pressing her wider until he could breathe in her scent. When she started to protest, he became even more curious. But there weren't any hidden changes there, even as he explored thoroughly. Very thoroughly!

When she cried out with pleasure from her first climax brought on by his exploration, he lifted himself higher, stripping off his clothes before moving between her legs.

"You're beautiful, Faye," he said, taking her hands and shifting so that she was on top of him. "Every inch of you is absolutely beautiful!"

"I'm fat now," she whispered, agonizing over his comments. But he didn't allow that. He simply started his exploration all over again, proving that he loved her new curves.

"You're not fat," he told her when he entered her this time, condom firmly in place to protect her. "You're absolutely beautiful. And even more lovely now because of the changes." He saw the moment she accepted his statement and slid deeper in her heat, being extra careful, wondering if she was tender after giving birth. She only hissed once and he backed away, gently moving back into her warmth. When she didn't hiss this time, he moved deeper and deeper.

Shifting inside of her, Zantar forced himself to hold back, to give her every bit of pleasure possible. He'd been so angry with her yesterday, but now, knowing what she'd gone through and why, he wanted to make it all up to her. She'd been trying to protect him! Damn her, the silly woman! The silly, beautiful, amazing…he couldn't think any longer, his mind and body absorbed in the intense pleasure surrounding him. He could only feel now. Feel and absorb her cries of happiness. When he felt her getting closer, Zantar reached down, sliding his thumb against that nub to bring her closer because he couldn't hold back any longer. She just felt too good!

When he felt her shivers of release, only then did he allow himself to climax as well. He had no idea why, but this time, it was a thousand times better! Maybe because he knew that she loved him. Or maybe it was because she was here, in his bed and he didn't have to wonder where she would be next week or next month. She was his.

When it was all over, Zantar pulled her over until she was resting against his chest, staring up at the ceiling while he tried to catch his breath.

"Are you okay?" he asked, brushing his fingertips down her spine.

She laughed, but snuggled closer to him. "Yes."

"I hurt you initially, didn't I?"

She stiffened, then turned her face, kissing his chest. She didn't answer for a long time until he finally lifted his head, looking down at her. "Faye?"

"I'm fine," she told him, acting as if that were the end of the conversation.

He rolled over, looking down at her. "What's wrong?"

She looked up at him, her fingers tangling in his hair. "Nothing is wrong," she said, her voice barely above a whisper. "It was absolutely beautiful!" She shifted her leg so that she more perfectly cradled his body. "When are we supposed to be married?"

He groaned, then looked at his watch. "About an hour ago."

He laughed when she leapt out of bed, then dove for cover when she remembered that she was completely naked. She merely grabbed his shirt and rushed into the bathroom.

Zantar followed at a more leisurely pace, more than ready to delay the wedding for another hour.

Epilogue

"You were going too fast," Faye grumbled as she waddled down the sidewalk towards the horse and pony that had come to a dusty halt by the fence.

"Define too fast," Zantar laughed, walking over to lift four-year-old Shanta off of her pony. The energetic toddler was already halfway to the ground, but her father lifted her up and gave her a tickle on her tummy.

Faye shook her head but couldn't stop smiling at the two. Father and daughter were too much alike. Shanta loved her daddy and tried to keep up with everything he did. She even sat in on council meetings at times, her tiny features wrinkled with concentration as she tried to understand everything that was being discussed.

At the moment though, she was wiggling to get down and Zantar lowered her tiny, boot covered feet to the ground. Moments later, Shanta rushed over, placing both of her hands on Faye's rounded tummy. "Is he awake, Momma?" she asked, then pressed her ear against Faye's stomach. "Are you awake, little brother?"

Her face squinched up into a frown when she didn't hear anything or feel her unborn brother move around in Faye's stomach.

"He's sleeping," Shanta announced, then moved back, reaching her arms up in a silent command to her father to lift her into his arms. Of course, Zantar lifted Shanta up because...well, because he adored her and spoiled his sweet daughter.

"How are you?" he asked Faye, reaching down with his free hand to cover her belly. "You didn't sleep well last night."

Faye sighed, nodding her head. "I know." She lifted her face up. "I love you. But if you don't stop racing across the desert with our daughter, I'm going to have to hurt you."

He laughed, obviously not worried about her dire threat. "You should be in bed."

"I'm bored in bed. I want chocolate chip cookies."

Zantar rolled his eyes, but Shanta clapped her hands.

"Let's go then," he said, restraining their daughter from flying over to her mother. "Kitchen it is!"

"I love Momma's cravings!" Shanta called out.

Zantar put an arm around her waist, kissing her neck. "I do too!"

Faye smiled, leaning her head against his shoulder. "My cravings," she teased, "are what got us into this predicament," she said, referring to her bulging belly.

"I know. Have I mentioned that I love you?"

Faye smiled, her irritation at his speed on their horses gone. "I love you too!"

Postlogue

"I'm proud to introduce all of you to Doctor Faye Lafayette. Her groundbreaking research into the previously unknown artist, Agari Tismona, shed significant light into the fascinating culture of fourteenth century life in Skyla." The man smiled as the audience applauded enthusiastically. "Without further introduction, I give you, Dr. Lafayette!"

The applause was thunderous as Faye stepped out onto the stage. She walked over to the podium, adjusted the microphone and tried very hard not to look out at the audience. Clearing her throat, she paused a moment to look over to the left. There he was. Zantar stood just off-stage, watching her, his harsh features not smiling, but she could see the pride in his eyes.

And that was all it took. Her confidence skyrocketed and she turned back to the audience. All of her stage fright seemed to dissipate simply because Zantar was here with her.

"Thank you for that warm welcome," she greeted everyone, then clicked the button. Behind her, an enormous picture of one of Tismona's paintings lit up the stage.

"This is the painting most people ask about. The gardenia floating in the water," she clicked the button again to show the magnified area of the painting, "and the strange box. Both are floating in what looks to be a calm sea." She continued, flipping through the small aspects of the painting that didn't make much sense. "After reading hundreds of letters from that time period, I've come to the conclusion that the gardenia represented Princess Floria al Sintara, the daughter to King Dimirt al Sintara, who reigned during the years fourteen-twenty-five to fourteen-fifty-one. Floria was betrothed to the prince in the neighboring region, but this was not a love match, according to several letters that teemed with gossip. The box, in my opinion, represents the al

Sintara palace. In the painting, it is floating away. The seas look calm, but if you focus your attention here," she clicked the button again, "it appears that a storm is brewing in the distance." Faye turned back to the audience, gratified that everyone seemed to be entranced by the paintings and her findings. Several people were even taking notes. "In this painting, again, everything seems peaceful. But look more closely on the wall outside through this window." Another click, and the small map appeared. "After scouring maps from various countries, I finally discovered that this map leads to another area of the world that has since been transformed into an urban center." She clicked on the new map, with the old painting-map side by side. "The details are scant, but references to several letters and a historian's detailing of a battle led me to believe that this was the road that Princess Floria would take to escape from her unwanted betrothal."

Faye continued, lecturing on the various symbols in the paintings. By the end of the ninety-minute lecture, she brought everything back. "So you can see how one woman's battle for freedom is at the basis for the fall of the al Sintara kingdom."

The audience was stunned for a long moment, then everyone cheered, standing up as they clapped their appreciation for her research and explanation.

Once again, Faye turned, finding Zantar's eyes. There he was. Always her rock! No hidden map for her, she thought. Her way was right there, stage left!

A message from Elizabeth:
This book wasn't supposed to be a part of this series. Originally, there were only three books to this series and I can't really tell you why or how Zantar and Faye's story came into being. I wish I was more "sane" about my writing process. However, very often, I get a crazy niggle and just have to write the story. Hence, this book! I hope that you enjoyed this romance, even though Faye isn't technically part of the Del Taran family. I justified including this book in the series because Zantar was a friend of the family.

And now for my usual plea for reviews! Someone commented that it takes longer than a few seconds to type out a review and I laughed. Apparently, I type a wee bit faster than the average person. So...could you take a moment to leave me a review? Return to the retailer site to the book review page – and I thank you!

(As usual, if you don't want to leave feedback in a public forum, feel free to e-mail me directly at elizabeth@elizabethlennox.com. I answer all e-mails personally, although it sometimes takes me a while. Please don't

be offended if I don't respond immediately. I tend to lose myself in writing stories and have a hard time pulling my head out of the book.)
 Elizabeth
 (Keep scrolling for a fun excerpt from next month's "Her Forbidden Sheik"!)

ELIZABETH LENNOX

Excerpt from "Her Forbidden Sheik"
Release Date: July 15, 2022

Nasir tried to appear calm as he stood at the foot of the stairs to the plane, waiting for Ayla. Unfortunately, the woman was late. Pacing back and forth, he went over the plans in his mind once again, trying to find areas where the bad guys might hurt Ayla.

Maybe he should just call this off. They could come up with another plan, he thought. If anything happened to Ayla, Nasir knew that he'd never forgive himself!

He was just lifting his phone out of his pocket when a line of SUVs drove onto the tarmac. A second later, there was a rush of reporters running across the tarmac towards him. His guards immediately stepped up, forming a line, but the reporters halted at the roped off area, pulling out their cameras and shoving their recorders into the air, yelling questions to him.

But the moment Ayla's SUV came to a stop, there was absolute silence. The reporters even forgot to lift their microphones while the cameras of the photographers remained limp in their hands. It was as if everyone's breath stopped for a moment, holding in their lungs as they waited for Princess Ayla to step out.

One beautiful red stiletto. Then a sexy calf. A dark skirt. A moment later, the rest of Ayla emerged from the SUV. That was their cue for the reporters to go nuts, all of them screaming out questions to Ayla, trying to be overheard over the din of the other questions.

For her part, Ayla took it all in stride. It was like she was a rock star, and the paparazzi were salivating for just a coy smile in their direction. She walked over to him and…he had the same reaction. His breath caught in his throat as he watched her walk over to her. Was she moving in slow motion on purpose? The smile she gave him…it was both a promise and dare. A challenge and a salacious gift that carried over the heated currents of air towards him.

And Ayla didn't just walk. She sauntered. Her hips swayed just enough to make a man's mind blank. Her silk blouse almost hugged her breasts, teasing him with the tantalizing knowledge of what was underneath. And her legs! Dear heaven, her legs were…too long for such a short woman! Nasir watched, his eyes taking in every detail of her red silk blouse and black skirt, her red shoes and…and her dark hair. Damn, her hair was pulled back into some sort of twist. He didn't like that. He preferred her hair to flow over her shoulders, tempting him to reach out and run his fingers through it.

It wasn't fair that she controlled him with just a walk and a smile.

He almost resented the woman for being so damned beautiful! And yet, she'd always had this kind of an impact on him. For years, he'd watched her, lusted for her, respected her, and knew that she would grow into just this kind of woman.

"Good morning, Your Highness," Ayla said with a sultry smile to her red lips.

"You look beautiful, Ayla," he said, taking her hand and lifting her fingers to his lips.

Ayla trembled as his lips touched her fingertips, trying to hide the shiver of awareness. She wanted to jerk her hand away, not let him know the power he had over her. Since stepping out of the vehicle, she'd had eyes only for Nasir. He was so tall, dark, and powerfully handsome. He compelled her. He pulled her in, like a giant magnet and she was the steel. Ayla knew that she should have gone over to the reporters and answered some of their questions. But as soon as she'd seen Nasir standing here at the base of the stairs, there had been no other action other than to walk to him.

And now she stood here, not sure what to do. Not sure what to say. How could he have this kind of power over her? Why did she turn into a tongue-tied school girl whenever she was around this man?

What had he said? Something about her looks. "Thank you," she whispered, lowering her lashes because she just couldn't take the intensity in his eyes now. She'd thought she was prepared for this. For him! But standing here now, feeling her knees wobble, Ayla was terrified of falling on her face. Wouldn't that be a good headline for tonight's news? *"Princess Falls at the Sheik's Feet!"* Oh, that would definitely go viral!

"I guess we should get on with it?" she offered.

Printed in Great Britain
by Amazon